A CHRISTMAS AFFAIR TO REMEMBER

A Longhope Abbey Holiday Novella

MIA VINCY

A Christmas Affair to Remember

Ebook ISBN: 978-1-925882-10-0

Print ISBN: 978-1-925882-11-7

CONTENT NOTES: *Past death of a spouse, financial hardship, infidelity*

Cover design: Studio Bukovero

Development Editing: May Peterson

This book was written on the lands of the Dja Dja Wurrung people, and I acknowledge them as Traditional Owners. I pay my respects to their Elders, past and present, and the Aboriginal Elders of other communities.

A CHRISTMAS AFFAIR TO REMEMBER

NOTE ON LANGUAGE

In the context of this story, "cordials" are like flavored liqueurs, often made by distillation, and purported to have medicinal qualities.

CORDIAL:
1. A medicine that increases the force of the heart, or increases the circulation.
2. Any medicine that increases strength.
3. Anything that comforts, gladdens and exhilarates.

— SAMUEL JOHNSON'S *A DICTIONARY OF THE ENGLISH LANGUAGE* (1792)

Guide to pronunciation of English place names:
Warwickshire = wo-ruhk-shuh
Worcestershire = wu-stuh-shuh

CHAPTER 1

When Sylvia had predicted that the expedition to gather Christmas greenery would end with a lady stuck in a tree, needing to be rescued by Mr. Isaac DeWitt, she had only been joking. She hadn't imagined for a heartbeat that any of the ladies would actually get stuck.

She had certainly not imagined that *she* would get stuck.

Yet here she was, wedged midair with one foot on a stone wall, the other on a tree trunk, her legs stretched so wide and straight she could go neither forward nor backward, nor up nor down.

And there he was, Isaac DeWitt, laughing up at her with his flashing dark eyes.

"What a lovely sightseeing spot you've found, Mrs. Ray," he said lazily. "How's the view from up there?"

"Quite marvelous," she replied, striving for nonchalant tones despite the growing protest of her mistreated legs. "I begin to understand the appeal of the countryside."

The view was indeed lovely. Before her stretched peaceful expanses of woodlands and rolling green hills, divided by hedges and dotted with denuded trees. In one direction rose the steeple of the village church, and in another lay the rambling red-brick Tudor manse known as Sunne Park, where Sylvia was the guest of Lady Charles Lightwell and her daughter and son-in-law, Cassandra and Joshua DeWitt.

Up on the highest hill, the ruins of Longhope Abbey were outlined against the wintry sky. The sky was gray, but the clouds seemed to shimmer and sparkle, and the air was cold, but it was invigorating and clean.

Besides, Sylvia wore the fur-lined hat and gloves and thick forest-green coat that Lady Charles had gifted her; after several winters of shivering and cursing, she had forgotten how enjoyable cold weather could be when one was sufficiently protected against it. The winter clothes may be her friend's castoffs, but they were the most deliciously decadent items Sylvia had owned since she was a girl.

"What do you think of the countryside, Mr. Isaac?" she asked. "Are you enjoying the view?"

Her skirts had bunched up during her little misadventure, so he was surely getting a nice eyeful of her calves in their muddy boots and thick woolen stockings.

"More and more all the time," he drawled, his lips twitching with the promise of one of his devilish smiles. "Some say the country is dull, but that's not my experience today."

Then the tiniest frown skittered across his face. He took off his hat and looked down at it thoughtfully. Several long strands of his dark hair escaped the leather thong tied at his nape to brush against the firm angle of his jaw. A moment later, apparently resolved to something, he smoothed back his hair, replaced his hat, and looked up at her again.

"Certainly, it is enlivened by this conundrum before me —a double conundrum," he said. "First, the puzzle of how you arrived in that unusual position. Second, the puzzle of how I am to bring you back down to earth without placing my hands on your person in a manner that will heat your daydreams for weeks."

Sylvia clutched her basket and took a quick gulp of that clean, cold, invigorating air. It was many years since a man had put his hands on her person, and she'd not allowed herself to think about how much she missed things like that. She'd had no opportunity to be the proverbial Merry Widow, having directed all her energy toward being the Not-Starving Widow. And she was soon to be married again, she reminded herself. Although Graham Ossett showed no interest in her body, which, honestly, was something of a relief.

She looked away from Isaac DeWitt's tempting hands, up at the tempting balls of bright-green mistletoe clustered around the bare branches of the tree above her.

Temptation: *That* was what had landed her in this position, the temptation of all that lovely mistletoe. More than that, to be honest: the temptation of proving she could harvest it herself, because she was very good at doing things herself and she did not need dashing, vigorous young men with rakish charm and flashing dark eyes to do things for her.

Sounds of laughter and chatter from the rest of their boisterous party floated over the field. It was a large party, thirteen in total, accompanied by the grooms with the donkey cart, plus Mr. Joshua DeWitt's two dogs. She'd left the group under an even bigger tree, also covered in big balls of mistletoe—a tree that Mr. Isaac had recently climbed, to everyone's very vocal admiration.

When the party had come to the tree, Miss Prudence

Babworth had stared longingly up at the mistletoe and then stared longingly at Mr. Isaac. Her younger sister Miss Lettie Babworth had made a few futile attempts to jump at the lower branches.

"We need someone to climb the tree for us," Miss Babworth had said, her gaze lingering on Mr. Isaac, before she remembered herself and extended her appeal to the other gentlemen in the party. There was Mr. Joshua DeWitt, who was attached to his wife with one hand and brandishing a stick in the other, which he occasionally threw for his dogs to fetch. The other options were Mr. DeWitt's new investment partner, Lord Tidcombe, whose air of lethargy suggested he had no ambitions to climb anything taller than a sofa, and the three inventors who, as usual, were engaged in intense conversation and ignored the rest of the group. The engineers' names were Fadden, Ford, and Frye, and even after a fortnight at the same house party, Sylvia had yet to figure out which was which.

It was Emily Lightwell who had brightly nominated Mr. Isaac for the task.

"I say Isaac and Joshua should both climb," she had suggested. "Then we can bet on them, like a donkey race."

To which the elder Mr. DeWitt retorted: "Donkeys can't climb trees. And if you ladies want mistletoe, you can stop blithering about down here and climb the blasted trees yourselves."

"Joshua," his wife Cassandra admonished gently. "The ladies cannot climb trees in those long dresses."

His jaw dropped; his eyes widened. "Mrs. DeWitt!" he said. "You're not suggesting the ladies take off their dresses? I am shocked."

Cassandra DeWitt laughed softly and said, "You know I said nothing of the sort," at which they regarded each other with such affection that Sylvia had to look away.

Which meant she had not missed a minute of Mr. Isaac's actions, as he shucked off his greatcoat and hat, flashed a devilishly handsome grin at the ladies—well, not at Sylvia, but at the Babworth sisters, Emily Lightwell, Jane Newell, and Miss Vincent—and said, "I'll show you how it's done."

Then he had scampered up the tree's branches like a man born to it. Or rather, like a man who had joined the Navy as a boy and spent his formative years shinnying up masts and dancing across the rigging.

Once he had made himself comfortable on a branch, he drew a knife from his boot and sliced off great gorgeous clumps of mistletoe, which he tossed down to where Emily, Jane, Prudence, and Lettie waited below. The four young ladies bounced around like puppies, making a game of catching the mistletoe and tossing it onto the branches of pine and other greenery already in the cart, while the grooms gathered up the bits they missed and the donkey twitched its big ears with a philosophical air.

Sylvia had watched Mr. Isaac helplessly, because there was something so *watchable* about that sort of vigor and competence, that easy assurance of a young man hauling himself up a tree without hesitation, flashing that grin and taking care to aim his parcels of mistletoe so each girl caught a fair share.

Yes, of all the family and guests, it should have been one of the Babworth sisters in need of rescuing. Prudence Babworth had a good head on her shoulders, but her infatuation with Mr. Isaac was making her silly. At first, Miss Babworth had been subtle, but she had become increasingly obvious as the target of her affections remained stubbornly oblivious. Mr. Isaac smiled and flirted with her, of course, but he smiled and flirted with everyone.

Or the younger sister Miss Lettie might have needed rescuing, for she was already silly and, it was said, fast becoming the biggest flirt in the parish of Longhope Abbey. Or high-spirited Emily Lightwell with her head in the clouds, or her placid friend Jane Newell with her feet firmly on the ground, or even the inscrutable governess, Miss Vincent.

Indeed, the only lady on the expedition less likely than Sylvia to need rescuing by Isaac was Cassandra DeWitt, and that was because Cassandra was too ladylike to climb a tree in the first place, and if she did, it would be her own husband who did the rescuing.

At any rate, it ought never to have been sensible, pragmatic widow Sylvia Ray who got stuck. In all her thirty-three years, Sylvia had never so much as attempted to climb a tree, if only because she was a Birmingham girl; while the city of Birmingham was famous for making metal and making money, it was not known for making trees.

And, naturally, of all the men in the party, only one was a candidate for gallant rescuer.

That gallant rescuer sauntered closer. "If you'd allow me to make an observation, Mrs. Ray, it's that you are not what we would call tall."

"I have observed that about myself once or twice, Mr. Isaac."

"Yet despite your lack of height, you attempted to pick some mistletoe yourself."

She tried again to move her legs, but they refused to budge. "When one is short, one learns tricks to compensate for the lack of height."

"One trick favored by ladies is to make use of any tall men in the vicinity."

"I prefer to put my faith in more reliable objects. Such as ladders and boxes."

"And stone walls?" he offered dryly, gesturing at the wall whose treachery had landed her in this mess.

He stood right by her now. She could upend her basket over his head and shower him with its contents: glossy holly, spiky pinecones, and no mistletoe at all. Not that there was any need for her to gather more mistletoe, given his contribution. But Sylvia had felt compelled to harvest her own. Just to prove she could. Just to prove she didn't care he hadn't thrown any mistletoe down to her.

He inspected the position of her feet thoughtfully. "My guess is you climbed onto that stone wall with the aim of reaching up to pick the mistletoe. Very clever. Very resourceful. Except the wall, proving even less reliable than the tall men of your acquaintance, had a loose stone, which caused you to lose your balance. To save yourself from falling, you stepped out your other foot, but the only thing to balance yourself on was the tree trunk. And so here you are, one foot on the wall, one foot on the tree, and unable to move. How am I doing?"

Sylvia flexed her thighs and sighed. "An excellent reconstruction of events. I understand why the businessmen of Birmingham speak so highly of your investigative skills."

"They also speak highly of my resourcefulness, but we now return to the problem of how I am to rescue you without putting my hands all over you. I'm given to understand that's not at all the thing."

Drat, darn, and curses. There was something so wretchedly appealing about him, with his vigor and cocky charm and too-long hair, and there was something so very annoying about him, because she had a weakness for charming, confident men. But a woman could afford only one such weakness in a lifetime, and she had already married and buried hers.

How she envied those young ladies, openly admiring him. She missed being young. Not that thirty-three was old, not objectively, but in comparison to twenty, it was verily ancient. She missed being able to look at a handsome charmer like Isaac DeWitt and enjoy him for what he was, rather than tally up all the things he wasn't.

"I don't need rescuing," she lied.

He folded his arms and shrugged. "Then I'll wait until you sort yourself out. I'm fascinated to see what you do next."

"Very well," she conceded. "Maybe I need a bit of rescuing."

He cocked his head. His lips twitched once, twice. She waited but, alas, he did not succumb to a smile.

"If the thought of my manhandling you is the problem, we could unhitch the donkey and position it underneath you, and then you could drop—plop!—onto its back. That way I wouldn't have to touch you."

She did wish he would stop talking about touching her.

"Plopping onto a donkey's back sounds decidedly uncomfortable," she said. "I doubt the donkey would enjoy it much either."

"Chances are, the poor thing would bolt, and off you'd go, hurtling across the country, and you'd be found three days later in Yorkshire. Have you ever ridden a donkey?"

"I've never had that pleasure. But then, I've never had the pleasure of being stuck against a tree either. No one ever warned me the country was so fraught with danger."

"Then it seems the lesser danger is for me to manhandle you. You're small enough. I'll just toss you over my shoulder."

"I'd advise against it." She gestured at him with her

basket. "You're favoring one leg. It seems you hurt yourself, all that climbing up and down trees."

"An old injury. It's fine," he said absently, with a dismissive flick of his fingers.

He took her basket and placed it on the wall, then set his hat on top of her crop of pinecones and holly.

"Your legs must be aching," he said, coming to stand beside her. "Not that I should mention that, as I'm given to understand that a gentleman never mentions a lady's body parts in that lady's presence. But then, I don't qualify as a gentleman, and I can't get past the fact that you do indeed have legs, and this would prove a difficult situation to navigate if we're both forced to pretend you don't. May I?"

Her legs were indeed aching. She feared they would never bend again. "Please do."

"A woman who begs," he murmured. "My favorite."

Such terrible lines would not win him any poetry contests, but there was that warmth in his expressive dark eyes, and those broad shoulders now in line with her hips, and there was something in his words and tone that took her back, back to wondrous sensations she'd not felt in years.

An inconvenient frisson rippled through her, and she snapped, irritably, "Have you ever met anyone with whom you did not flirt?"

He raised an eyebrow. "Are you opposed to flirting, Mrs. Ray? And if so, is it only you who is not to flirt, or do you mean to ban it for everyone?"

"Of course not," she said, suddenly confused. "It's not the flirting that bothers me. It's that you flirt with every lady indiscriminately, with nothing but empty, pointless charm."

"Ah, so that's why," he said, as if to himself. "I sensed your aversion to me when you first arrived, and so I kept

9

my distance, though I didn't understand the cause. But now we have it: I am nothing but empty, pointless charm."

Something entered his expression, not quite hurt or offense, but a soft, almost vulnerable look, at odds with his usual confidence. It made her want to soothe him, which, in the circumstances, irritated her all the more.

"Do not mistake me for one of those impressionable girls, Mr. Isaac. I know men like you: all spicy steam and no plum pudding."

Her words were unkind; she regretted them immediately. But to her surprise, he laughed, a laugh that sounded good-natured and, if she was not mistaken, a touch rueful.

"I believe I can say with certainty that you have never met a man quite like me."

"I insulted you. It was badly done. Forgive me."

He shook his head. "You spoke plainly, and you have no idea how much I appreciate that. And out of that appreciation, I'll not leave you here as you deserve, but will rescue you nonetheless."

Again he stepped closer, the wind teasing his very touchable hair. A new smile touched his lips. This smile was not flirtatious but secret and amused, as if he was privy to a joke that he would not share.

Sylvia had no chance to wonder what he meant before he pressed one solid shoulder into her abdomen and clamped one strong arm around her thighs. She immediately wobbled and balanced herself as best she could, which meant one hand landing on his head, the other on his upper back. He grunted but held his ground, lifting her up so she could pull her legs free and then stepping away.

He kept holding her like that, propped against his shoulder, facing behind him. She managed to take her hand off his head and rested it instead on his upper back. It was not a dignified position, up in the air like a clumsy opera dancer, but all that mattered were her poor legs. Tentatively, she bent her knees, which had been forced straight for too long, and groaned with pleasure at the relief.

"Oh, but that feels good," she moaned. "I feared I might never bend them again."

With another grunt, he turned. The movement caused her hands to slip and slide down the oiled fabric of his greatcoat, down his back, until she was bent double over his shoulder, looking down at the grass, held firm by that arm around her legs.

He retrieved her basket and set off back toward the party, with Sylvia slung over his shoulder like a sack of animal feed, her knees still bent.

"Mr. Isaac?" she called, as his long smooth strides bore them along, though her only view now was the flapping hem of his greatcoat and his footprints appearing in the grass behind them. "You can put me down now."

He only tightened his grip. "Your legs will be sore and tired, so you'll need to rest them before you try to walk. But do take care not to kick me."

"You'll be lucky if I don't kick you," she muttered, which threat he greeted with a light laugh. "A kick is looking more and more likely all the time."

CHAPTER 2

Isaac knew he should set Mrs. Ray down on the ground instead of hauling her across the countryside slung over his shoulder like a dockworker hauling a sack, but some devil prompted him to ignore her protests and carry on.

It was his first time carrying a woman in this manner, but it was not terrible. Sylvia Ray was not overly tall, nor overly heavy, and their position was not overly awkward, even with her knuckles pressed into his back and her rounded rump, covered in forest-green wool, right beside his face. He wouldn't be able to carry her like this for miles —not with his bad leg suffering from the dual effects of the cold and his idiotic tree-climbing antics—but it wasn't far back to the others, and he suspected her own legs needed time to recover.

She'd been stuck in that uncomfortable position for longer than necessary, for which Isaac's hesitation to act was to blame. He should have helped her down sooner, should have grabbed her as soon as he came upon her, rather than indulging in a chat. But he had delayed due to, first, her general unexplained aversion to him, and secondly, his own nervousness about putting his hands on a woman, especially a woman who admitted to not liking him very much.

All spicy steam and no plum pudding.

Ah, wise Mrs. Ray, he thought. *You have no idea how right you are.*

It was Cassandra who noticed them first, her face stiffening with alarm.

"Isaac?" she cried, dashing toward him, drawing the attention of the group, so even Lord Tidcombe and the oblivious inventors stopped talking to stare. "What's happened to Mrs. Ray?"

"I'm quite fine, Mrs. DeWitt," came his cargo's voice from behind him. "If Mr. Isaac might be so kind as to put me down now."

"Isaac!" Cassandra's expression turned scolding. "What's going on? You mustn't haul ladies around like sacks of potatoes."

"I'm hauling her around like a sack of greenery, which is the entire purpose of this outing," Isaac protested with mock innocence. "I plucked her out of a tree, and now I shall toss her into the donkey cart with the rest of the greenery, and the girls can turn her into garlands and kissing boughs."

He grinned at Cassandra, and Joshua grinned at him.

"Carrying women upside down gets too much blood in their brains and then they develop ideas," Joshua said. "You must be careful about letting women develop ideas, because they've already got more than enough going on in those devious brains of theirs."

"This is very true," came Mrs. Ray's voice. "Thanks to the extra blood in my brain, I've developed ideas about giving Mr. Isaac a jolly good kick."

The others had gathered in a circle to watch them, enjoying these antics as if they were part of the Christmas festivities. Shaking her head, Cassandra took the basket from his hand, while Isaac tried to work out how to get Mrs. Ray down onto the ground without injuring her modesty or putting his hands all over her again. But she was of compact size and manageable weight, so he was able to more or less lift her up and off him, almost as if he were lifting her in a dance. After her feet touched the ground, he kept holding her elbows—elbows being, he had learned, one of the safer parts of a lady's body—and just as well, for her knees buckled and she clutched at his forearms.

Their eyes met. He thought he saw something in her gaze that lent a different flavor to her disapproval of him. As if she did like him but didn't want to like him.

But surely that was just his fancy. Women were exceedingly confusing. Isaac liked women, and women seemed to like him, but as for actually understanding them? Impossible. Ladies seemed to change their minds constantly, and have feelings he didn't know about, and rules he didn't understand, and they hardly ever said what they meant. According to Cassandra, ladies didn't mean to confuse him, but they were raised *not* to express themselves plainly, which was unfortunate, because Isaac would fare much better with women—particularly in his search for a wife—if there could be a bit more plain speaking all around.

Once she had found her legs, he moved aside to let Cassandra fuss over her and help her tidy her coat and hat.

"Mrs. Ray was stuck in a tree," Isaac explained to the array of intrigued faces.

"I wasn't quite *in* a tree," she amended good-naturedly. "I climbed onto a wall to pick mistletoe and then… It all happened rather quickly, but somehow I got stuck between the wall and the tree."

A wistful sigh poured out of Miss Lettie Babworth. "And Mr. Isaac rescued you."

"Idiot thing to do," Joshua said. "Half of Longhope Abbey is already infatuated with you, Isaac, it's like some bloody contagious fever. Now every lady for miles around will climb a tree in the hope you'll rescue her. There'll be women stuck up trees all over the place."

Miss Lettie clapped her hands. "And then Mr. Isaac will rescue us all!"

"Why the blazes would he do that?" Joshua shot back. "If a woman is foolish enough to get stuck in a tree, then it's the best place for her."

Mrs. Ray laughed. "As one of those foolish women, I must disagree with you, Mr. DeWitt. Much longer and my legs would have turned to wood and birds would have nested in my hair."

She seemed to have recovered. Isaac's hat was still in her basket; she handed it back to him.

"Please forgive my lack of gratitude," she said. "Truly, I am grateful for your assistance."

"Have you sufficiently recovered from your tree-climbing adventures?" he asked her, as he smoothed back his hair and replaced his hat. "Or shall I sling you over my shoulder again to haul you back to the house?"

She gave him a shrewd, amused look. "I think you're punishing me for the plum pudding comment."

"Maybe I just enjoy carrying you about. Like a child with a doll, I shall carry you about and play with you."

"There it is again," she sighed. "The flirting. The charm. The good looks."

"Is that a problem, Mrs. Ray?" Emily asked.

As she spoke, she gave Isaac's shoulder a sisterly bump.

Isaac nudged her back. Having adoptive sisters never grew boring; thanks to Joshua's marriage, Isaac had acquired three of them—Cassandra, Emily, and Lucy—as well as an adoptive mother in Lady Charles.

"Don't you like flirtatious, charming, good-looking men?" Emily added.

"Oh, I have a terrible prejudice against them," Mrs. Ray said cheerfully. "I married one, you see."

"What does that mean?" whispered one of the Babworths. "I don't know. I don't understand," whispered the other.

But Isaac understood. At least, he thought he did. Mrs. Ray held his gaze steadily. Her eyes were a mix of blue and green, her hair a mix of red and brown. Her expression was a mix of sorrow and rue and defiance and amusement and a thousand other things that rendered the widow very interesting indeed.

Upon her arrival at Sunne Park a fortnight earlier, she had borne a worn, tired look. Isaac had guessed her age to be closer to forty than thirty. When Lady Charles and Cassandra were settling her in her bedchamber, a couple of doors down from his, he'd overheard her proclaiming her intention to spend half her time in bed, the other half lazing by the fire, and all the time eating too much. Certainly, she managed to eat astonishing amounts of food for someone her size, but the rest must have been a joke, for in truth she was one of those people who delighted in being active and busy. She spent her days with Lady Charles, pottering about in the herb garden and brewing up devil knew what in the still room, and in the evenings, she threw herself whole-heartedly into whatever parlor game the ladies chose. Bit by bit, she had lost that pinched look and weary air. Her cheeks had become rounder, her movements quicker, her conversation livelier. Now he would put her age closer to thirty than forty. Indeed, now he thought about it, Mrs. Ray was quite attractive, for an older woman, with her heart-shaped face cozy under the rabbit fur of her hat, and that little dent in her chin, and the color in her cheeks from the exercise and, he supposed, from being carried upside down.

All of which piqued his irrepressible curiosity. How had she earned that worn, pinched look, and what did her charming, good-looking, and now dead husband have to do with it? He wanted to ask, but even he knew better than to insert dead husbands into pleasant, polite conversation.

"I believe I've met your father-in-law. Henry Ray, isn't it?" he asked instead. "A solicitor in Birmingham."

She gave one of those tight smiles ladies gave when they didn't want to talk about something. "That's him." She paused. "We don't speak much."

"By 'not much' you mean 'not at all,'" he guessed.

Another small pause. "Not since Michael's funeral a few years ago."

Now Isaac was definitely intrigued. Henry Ray was a wealthy man who gave as much to charity as anyone in his position, yet his widowed daughter-in-law had arrived here in a threadbare coat looking like she'd not had a decent meal in years; even now, if Isaac was not mistaken, she was wearing Lady Charles's clothes from two winters ago. A picture was emerging, but some pieces were missing, and Isaac had discovered pleasure, aptitude, and a lucrative business in finding missing pieces and making them fit.

But now was no time for interrogation, not when they stood outside on Christmas Eve, with a cartload of greenery, an impatient donkey, and an audience of curious young ladies.

"Well, have we enough greenery for your kissing

boughs?" he said to the group at large. "Can we go home, or do you need me to climb another tree?"

"Climb another tree," Emily ordered. "But carry me up with you this time. I'll ride on your back."

"Oh, so I'm your donkey now, am I?" Isaac teased.

She grinned at him cheekily. "Are you saying you're a bit of an ass?"

That earned her a brotherly poke in the shoulder. He willed her to shut up before the other ladies echoed her idea. Despite his offer, he prayed no one expected him to climb another tree; his leg was already aching enough.

It was Cassandra who announced it was time to head home. They had made an impressive harvest, swathes of pine and laurel and holly, all now topped with the bright-green mistletoe.

"You still need time to make the kissing bough, if we are to hang it this evening for our Christmas Eve festivities," she pointed out.

"We're making more than one kissing bough," Emily said. "We're having a contest."

"We tossed a coin," Miss Babworth chimed in. "Lettie and I will make one in a crown shape, and Emily and Jane will make one in a sphere, and you must judge which is the winner, Mrs. DeWitt. Mr. Isaac and the other men have already made the frames for us to tie the greenery onto."

Jane Newell said, "There's enough greenery for more than two. Miss Vincent and Mrs. Ray could make a third kissing bough."

"And Cassandra, you and Mama can make a fourth one," Emily said.

"Sweet mercy," Joshua exploded. "At this rate, there'll be kissing boughs all over the house. Nothing will get done and we'll starve because everyone will spend all their time kissing. It'll be mayhem and terror. Terrible idea, kissing boughs."

Cassandra caught his arm. "What a shame. I planned to make a small one for our bedchamber, but if you don't approve…"

"Brilliant idea, kissing boughs," Joshua immediately said. "More of them the better. Especially in my bedchamber."

He grinned at his wife. Then, at a wave of his hand, one of the grooms took the donkey's bridle and coaxed it into grudging motion.

CHAPTER 3

The party split into twos and threes as they meandered along behind the donkey cart. Cassandra rode in the back of the cart with the mounds of greenery, facing backward, swinging her legs as she chatted to Joshua walking behind her.

"He *carried* her," Isaac heard Miss Lettie say to her sister behind him, in a whisper he suspected he was not meant to hear. "How marvelous. And how clever she must be, to arrange that. I could learn seduction techniques from her. You know what they say about widows."

"Lettie!" the elder Miss Babworth admonished in a low hiss. "Mrs. Ray is a respectable widow, not a courtesan. Don't speak of her thus. Besides, she's already engaged to someone else. And she's too old, anyway."

Isaac pretended he hadn't heard, as he veered off the track and into the woods. He forced himself to walk normally, though his leg ached in earnest now. Such foolish vanity, wanting to hide his weakness from those young ladies who had been so impressed by his athleticism. Mrs. Ray had noticed his limp, being the observant sort, but in her case, he didn't mind. She was not a young lady, nor a candidate for marriage; disappointing her was no concern, given she was so unimpressed with him as it was.

Learning seduction techniques, though. If only such a thing were possible. Lessons would save him the trouble of trying to figure out this seduction business himself. Not to mention the courting business. And, so help him, the kissing business.

What was he to do? Lurk under the kissing boughs to get practice and hope no one noticed how awkward and inept he was? Or hide out in a cabin in the woods until after the kissing boughs were taken down?

Kissing should be simple, surely. Seduction should be simple. Courtship should be simple.

Yet somehow, for Isaac, such simple things were proving devilishly hard.

His brother Joshua had done well for himself, he thought, as he scanned the woods for a stick that would serve as a staff to support his leg on the walk home. Joshua's marriage to Cassandra had been arranged by her late father, Lord Charles Lightwell, and the pair of them had not even spoken to each other for the first two years after their wedding. Yet here they were, deeply in love and wallowing in their happiness like a pair of pigs in mud.

An arranged marriage sounded like heaven, because then he could dispense with this tricky business of choosing a wife for himself.

Take Miss Prudence Babworth, for example. From what he knew of her, she would make him a good wife. She was twenty—the perfect age for him—and she was practical and responsible, with pretty, sand-colored hair and pleasant features. Her father was the land steward at Sunne Park, honest, reliable, and excellent at his job, and he even offered a decent dowry. Some might say Isaac would be marrying down, since he and Joshua were the sons of an earl, but they were the bastard sons of an earl, and while Joshua had married the granddaughter of a duke, Isaac was happy to avoid further connections to the aristocracy. He wanted a partner, a companion, a helpmate, not a fine lady he'd need to look after like a porcelain doll. Yes, Miss Babworth met his basic criteria; if only he knew what to do next.

He stopped walking—aha! That big stick, jutting out of a fallen log, would make a suitable staff. The stick was nearly as tall as he was and as thick as his wrist, and mostly straight. With a stomp of his boot he broke it off, then he stripped off the twigs poking out from it. He was so engrossed in his efforts that it was not until he had finished and was admiring his handsome staff that he noticed Prudence Babworth watching him from nearby. Her hands were behind her back, her eyes were wide, and she was biting her lip, looking very nervous.

No one else was around.

Isaac suddenly felt very nervous too.

"I've found you, Mr. Isaac," she said. "I worried you had wandered off and got lost."

"So you came to rescue me. How very gallant you are."

With what he interpreted as a coquettish look, she added, "I've heard it said that a rescuer gets a reward."

She didn't name the reward. Everyone knew the reward for gallantry was a kiss. Right. A kiss. Miss Babworth wanted a kiss. Which worked out nicely, because Isaac wanted a kiss too.

And this would be an excellent opportunity to figure out how kissing worked.

If there was any doubt about the matter, Miss Babworth stepped closer and revealed what she was hiding behind her back: a sprig of mistletoe, with bright-green leaves and little white berries.

"Look what I have," she nearly whispered and held up the sprig, her fingers in line with the top of her head.

Isaac draped both hands over his staff in a nonchalant manner and leaned on it, letting it take some of the weight off his aching leg. Prudence was of medium height— shorter than he was, taller than Mrs. Ray—and even though she held the mistletoe above her head, he would have to stoop to get below it. But then he would have to stoop to kiss her anyway, and did he stoop from the knees or just round his back? And then—

So help him, it was barely a month since his most recent attempt to kiss a woman, which had gone as badly as all his prior attempts. It had been outside an assembly in Manchester, where he'd been flirting with the woman, the sister of a business acquaintance. In a pause in the conversation, she had lifted her face to his and closed her eyes. So he had closed his eyes too and bent his head to kiss her—but instead just banged their noses quite painfully, and then their chins in his haste to escape, and then she had snapped, "What on earth do you think you're doing?"

And that had been that.

He would keep his eyes open, this time. Make sure he was certain of the location of Miss Babworth's mouth so he didn't miss. Perhaps he'd take her chin in his hands, hold her still, and that way avoid her nose.

He could do this.

He'd survived his family falling apart when he was ten. He'd survived a ship falling apart when he was eighteen. He'd survived his own life falling apart at twenty-four when the Navy gave him the boot because they had no use for a sailor with a gammy leg.

He could survive a kiss with Prudence Babworth without falling apart.

He looked at her mouth. He looked at her expectant eyes. He looked at the mistletoe.

"Did you pick that mistletoe yourself?" he heard himself say instead.

Her smile wavered. "It's from a bunch you threw down to me. When you climbed the tree. Which was ever so impressive."

"And, ah, mistletoe. Does it, ah, work outside? Or do the rules only apply inside the house?"

Her arm lowered. Distress crept over her face. "I don't think… The rules aren't actually the point."

"Of course not."

It was decided: He would take her face in his hand and hold her still. If she couldn't move, then he wouldn't bash in her nose or break her teeth or give her a concussion or anything like that.

But the air was cold. His glove would be cold too. Would she really want him to press cold, rough leather against her skin? And that cold leather would be dirty now also, from stripping the twigs off his staff. Then he would be not only freezing her but also smearing dirt on her face. If there were any instructions on how to kiss—and how he wished there were!—surely smearing dirt on the lady's face would be in the "Best avoid" list.

But if he didn't hold her face still, she might move and he'd end up shoving his nose in her eye or something, and his nose would be even colder than his leather glove.

The mistletoe had dropped to her shoulder level now.

"Do you decorate your own house with greenery every Christmas?" he asked desperately.

Her mouth wobbled, but she gamely said, "Of course. But not this year, as Mrs. DeWitt invited Lettie and me to stay at Sunne Park, with Mama and Papa traveling away."

He already knew that.

He looked at the mistletoe again. So did she. He looked at her pink face. He looked away.

Then she cried, "Oh, forget it" and flung the sprig of mistletoe at him and ran away through the woods.

With a groan of disgust at himself, Isaac pressed his hand over his face. His glove leather was indeed cold. It would have been like stroking her with an icicle.

Lowering his hand, he stared up at the wintry sky through the branches and breathed in the cold air. Now he'd have to face her over dinner every night for the next several weeks.

Behind him, a stick cracked.

He froze. She was back!

But when he spun around, he saw not Miss Babworth, but Mrs. Ray, mid-turn, her shoulders rounded and head ducked as if she was trying to be furtive, fleeing the scene like an inept thief. Another twig cracked under her foot. She froze, shot him a glance. Their eyes met.

She put him in mind of a woodland creature, in her coat and hat the color of pine needles, with the brown fur lining the collar and brim: bright-eyed, resourceful, observant, brimming with industrious energy.

But no woodland creature ever wore such an expression of embarrassment and pity. Damn the woman. She had witnessed his mortifying failure with Prudence Babworth, and she was worldly enough to have understood what she had seen.

"Enjoying the scenery again, Mrs. Ray?" he snapped. "You do find yourself in interesting positions today, don't you?"

His tone was harsh and unkind, but he couldn't stop it,

not when he was so embarrassed and angry and disgusted with himself. And there was something terrible about it being Mrs. Ray who had witnessed his failure, though a moment ago he'd been sure her opinion meant nothing to him.

Yet her expression only softened. Somehow, her kindness made it worse.

"Forgive me," she said, slightly breathless. "I didn't mean to intrude. I heard voices, so I... I didn't mean to witness..."

"What?" He gripped his staff harder. "What do you think you witnessed?"

"To be honest, I'm not sure."

He wanted her gone. He wanted to be alone. "It doesn't matter anyway. Go join the others."

With a thoughtful pause, she glanced in the direction of the trail, then looked back at him.

Then she lifted her skirts, stepped over a log, and headed his way.

MR. ISAAC STRAIGHTENED as Sylvia approached, his dark gaze wary.

She was not sure what possessed her to walk toward him, any more than she was sure what she had witnessed. But she was sure his anger was born out of embarrassment.

Something in his expression sparked her compassion: that lost, vulnerable look. True, her acquaintance with Mr. Isaac was no older than a fortnight, but until today, she had never seen him looking unsure.

He gripped his staff tightly, she noticed. During his conversation with Miss Babworth, he had relaxed against it, in a lazy manner that was so fetching in an athletic man. But having noticed his slight limp, she suspected his true purpose was to take some weight off an aching leg. Perhaps that was why he had not seized the opportunity to kiss Miss Babworth?

That was the part Sylvia did not comprehend. She had labeled him a rake, albeit a rake on his best behavior, as respect for Mrs. DeWitt and Lady Charles would prevent him from dallying with their guests.

So upon spying him alone with Miss Babworth she had —well. She was no prudish, self-appointed chaperone, for she didn't believe young ladies should be fenced off like mares in heat, but she had lingered, just in case Mr. Isaac responded dishonorably to Miss Babworth's clumsy, naive advance.

But no rake would have responded to a young lady's advance like that.

What was he? A conundrum, to use his own word.

"I think what I saw was Miss Babworth trying to coax a kiss from you, and you avoiding it."

That earned a bark of dry laughter. "Avoiding it? Failing, rather. Completely failing to kiss a willing woman." Then he frowned, and added, all in a rush, "She was willing, wasn't she? Am I wrong in thinking she wanted me to kiss her?"

"From what I witnessed, it looked very much like she wished for you to kiss her. The mistletoe was a rather strong hint," she added wryly.

If anything, he seemed even more bewildered. Unexpected fondness surged through her. She stepped close enough to lay her gloved hand over his on the staff. He didn't move.

"It must have been an awkward situation, but if you don't want to kiss a woman, you don't have to. She was being very forward. Both Babworth sisters have been behaving badly. I've come to expect it of Miss Lettie, but Miss Babworth has seemed more sensible until today. I imagine it must be difficult for a gentleman to turn down a lady, and it's kind of you to want to spare her feelings, but —and perhaps I'm speaking only for myself—it's better to state clearly to the woman that you don't feel that way about her."

He shook his head, releasing a rueful breath. "You sound very wise, but you have it all wrong. I'm not unwilling. Indeed, I welcomed Miss Babworth's advance and didn't wish to turn her down. It's that I'm…"

The words trailed off as he removed his hat with his spare hand, only to study it as if he hadn't the faintest idea what it was. Once more, those strands of hair that had escaped the tie at his nape drifted down his cheeks. An image of him suddenly swam into her mind: all his jaw-length hair loose and hanging around his face as he leaned over her. She shoved the vexing, unhelpful image away.

"I don't understand," she said. "Have you taken a vow of celibacy? Are you promised to someone else? You looked very disconcerted. Yet all across Longhope Abbey, your name is synonymous with rakish charm, wicked grins, and dizzying flirtation, and I swear you've won the affection of everyone in skirts, from the silly young ladies, to the sensible farmers' wives, to the vicar's ancient grandmother. You give every appearance of enjoying the presence of ladies, and they give every appearance of enjoying you right back."

"'Tis as you yourself said, Mrs. Ray. I'm all spicy steam and no plum pudding." A bitter, self-mocking tone edged his voice. "All hot air and no substance. All flirting and no kissing."

Sylvia once more regretted her earlier words, for it was

unfair to blame him for Michael's faults. She had not expected her insult to wound him so deeply he would quote it back at her.

"You flirt with everyone," she pointed out.

He shrugged. "It's habit now. When I left the Navy, restarted my life back on land, well, I hadn't a clue about women, but they seemed to like me. And I like women. I'd been living on ships since I was ten, and they never allow women on ships, so just having women in the same room was a revelation."

"Even older women like me?" she teased gently.

"All women. You all have this different perspective on life and you're all so…" He sighed. Then his eyes snapped to meet hers. "And you're not old," he added hastily. "You're… Well, you're…"

"I'm what?" She was enjoying his discomfort now, just a little, and it made her flirtatious, just a little. *Stop it*, she scolded herself, but she didn't. "I am older than you. Does that make me an ancient crone?"

"Neither ancient nor a crone. But you…" He waved his hat. "You're safe."

Well. That iced her flirtatious impulse. "I beg your pardon. I'm *safe*?"

He didn't seem to notice he had offended her. It was a mystery why she was even offended.

"You're engaged to be married, and you're older, and you disapprove of me." He snorted with amusement. "That is, you're too smart and worldly to be impressed by me. Flirting with you is safe. I can flirt with you and know you won't dangle sprigs of mistletoe over my head and expect me to kiss you or marry you or anything like that."

"Such menacing creatures they are, these young ladies armed with mistletoe and expectations," she said. "I'm still confused. You say you enjoy women, but you are wary of us too. Is kissing so terrible then?"

"Kissing." He spat out the word like a curse.

He stamped his staff on the ground once and studied the hole it left in the damp forest floor. Once more, his hair fell forward over his face. She wanted to smooth it back. Was that the sort of thing a woman did when she was *safe*? When a young man felt he could confide in her and flirt with her, because he knew he would never be called upon to kiss her or impress her. Sylvia was no one's idea of a seductress and had never even thought to question her own virtue or respectability, but suddenly it made her feel very dowdy and dull, for this man to call her *safe*.

Unreasonable to feel so piqued, but it seemed she had a little vanity left in her yet.

When he looked at her again, his warm eyes carried that lost, vulnerable expression.

"A kiss: It's overwhelming," he said quietly. "I understand the theory, but every time I've attempted to kiss someone it's ended in disaster, with bumped noses or cracked jaws. I guess it's the sort of thing men must learn when they're younger, and they can bumble and fumble and no one much minds, but I'm nearly twenty-seven and Miss Babworth would expect me to know what I'm doing. But I couldn't do it, because what if I did it badly? And how can I marry a woman if I revolt her with a kiss? Now I've thought about it too much because it's always gone badly before, and I worry about it going badly again, and then—"

Before Sylvia even knew what she was doing, she was standing on her toes, and sliding her palm over his cheek, and pressing her lips to his soft, warm mouth, and she was showing him just how simple and natural a kiss could be.

THE LEATHER GLOVE on Isaac's cheek was cold—he'd been right about that—but her mouth, oh, sweet saints, her mouth was warm.

And soft and gentle and yet assured, the touch of her lips holding him in place, as much as her palm and his surprise.

Surprise, because in the same heartbeat that their lips touched and held, exhilaration shot through him like a lightning bolt, opening a direct line from his mouth to his groin, via a dip in his stomach.

Her eyelids fluttered closed, so he closed his eyes too, and it was perfect and right and everything *fit*, with no banging of noses or clashing of teeth. For another heartbeat, she held them both there, and then her lips moved against his in a caress.

The most astonishing part, which his startled brain barely grasped, was that such a light caress could spark such wondrous sensations, sending them dancing through him with delicate promise and radiant heat.

Again, her lips moved against his, and then she was pulling away.

Cold air rushed into the space between them, but his lips were still warm, and his cheeks and body too. He opened his eyes. She stood some feet away now, clutching her basket in both hands, against the dappled background of the woods. Her expression was unreadable. A tight smile twisted her lips—oh, what glorious lips!—and her gaze wavered.

Then she sighed, a strangely sad sound, and when she spoke, self-mockery threaded through her words.

"As you see, kissing is not so difficult. I suspect you have worried about it too much and too long, given your early awkward experiences. You built up kissing in your mind as a terribly overwhelming quest, and all that thinking prevented you from just doing it."

"But I didn't—" He stopped short.

She waited. Then: "Didn't what?"

"Do anything."

She flicked a glance heavenward. "Yes. I noticed. Which is unfortunate, and I apologize. 'Tis not pleasant to be kissed by someone when you don't want them to kiss you. From my side, 'tis not pleasant to kiss someone who doesn't want to be kissed. But perhaps I've made my point, that kissing is not an enormous hurdle." She turned away. "And that I am not safe. Forgive me, Mr. DeWitt. I have intruded too long."

Back straight, she walked toward the edge of the woods, basket held stiffly. Isaac, frozen in place, watched her nimbly jump over a fallen branch and weave her way through the trees.

CHAPTER 4

"My dear Sylvia, Thank you for your kind inquiry after my health. The cold bothers me dreadfully, but your special cordial provides some relief. I benefit from a larger dose than your recommendation, taken half an hour earlier. Do amend your instructions to fit. ... My digestion has eased thanks to your broth, which Mrs. Yates chooses to make as her particular duty. Mrs. Yates is proving an excellent housekeeper. Your assistance in interviewing her was invaluable. ... I am suffering a new cough, caused by dust arising from redecoration of your future chamber. The loud workers disturb my nerves considerably. It is a dry cough, and I feel it—"

"Have you a love letter, Mrs. Ray?"

At the girlish inquiry, Sylvia looked up from Graham's letter. A giggling Miss Lettie darted into the still room, closely followed by Miss Babworth, Miss Lightwell, and Miss Newell.

Across the room, Lady Charles looked up from bottling her new lavender wine to smile indulgently at them all.

Sylvia could not help but smile too. How glossy and

bouncy and *young* they were, from Lady Charles's youngest daughter Miss Emily Lightwell, a slight redhead not yet seventeen, through to Miss Babworth, sandy-haired and mature at twenty. How lovely they were too, though each of them had bemoaned imaginary physical flaws at some point. As Lady Charles observed one evening, young people could not understand the astonishing beauty of their youth until it was gone. Not that Lady Charles's famed beauty had gone; she was nearing fifty, but even with gray in her dark hair and lines on her skin, she was still one of the loveliest women Sylvia had ever met.

Miss Babworth had seemed downcast on the walk back to the house, but making the kissing boughs had clearly restored her spirits.

It had been a delightful few hours, watching the young ladies negotiate and concentrate as they twisted greenery around the frames the men had made, and tied on apples, bonbons, and colored candles. Cassandra, Lady Charles, Sylvia, and Miss Vincent had sat nearby, with tea and cakes, offering advice that went ignored, while sewing garlands of holly, ivy, and ribbons to hang about the house.

Sylvia had not had to face Isaac again immediately after her ill-conceived kiss—such a relief!—but when she and Cassandra had carried their garlands to decorate the nursery, she'd been dismayed to see him there, with his elder brother.

The DeWitt brothers had been standing in front of an elaborate doll's house, discussing renovations to it as earnestly as if it were real. They had spoken softly, for baby Rose was asleep in her cradle under the window, though she remained undisturbed by the occasional chortles of delight from little Charlie, propped on Mr. DeWitt's hip, tugging happily at his father's messy hair.

When she and Cassandra had entered, Joshua DeWitt

had favored his wife with a broad grin. "This dollhouse is brilliant," he said. "Why did we never dig it out before?"

Cassandra kissed her husband's stubbled cheek and petted her son's head. "It'll be a few years yet before Rose is ready to play with dolls."

He jogged Charlie on his hip, making him chortle anew. "By the time she's ready, this will be the greatest dollhouse England has ever seen."

Sylvia had risked a glance at Mr. Isaac, but he had steadfastly ignored her existence as he set a tiny chair on his palm, proclaiming it adorable, at which the two brothers took to cooing over the miniature furniture.

"The dollhouse was mine," Cassandra had explained, while putting up the garlands. "My older sister Miranda and I played with it mostly."

"I had one as a girl, too," Sylvia had said. She wasn't sure where it was now. She and Michael had never had children—a disappointment at first, later a bittersweet relief—so she'd never given her old dollhouse a thought. Her parents must have sold it along with everything else when they moved to Canada.

It hadn't been as fine as this one, but she had adored it all the same. A universal experience, perhaps, given Mr. Isaac's obvious—and charming—delight with the toy.

She shoved away thoughts of Isaac DeWitt and smiled brightly at the Babworth sisters, who were staring greedily at her letter from Graham. Graham had never kissed her. He had done no more than touch her hand, and that was only to guide her fingers to his pulse, which he feared was dangerously uneven; he had remained unconvinced by her assurances that his pulse felt quite robust.

But then, both she and Graham knew, tacitly at least, that their future marriage had nothing to do with kissing.

"Is the letter from your betrothed?" Miss Babworth

asked, more sedately and politely than her sister. "Mr. Ossett, did you say his name was?"

"That's right. Mr. Graham Ossett, of Kemble Manor in Worcestershire."

"A manor," sighed Miss Lettie.

Emily rolled her eyes. "Can someone *please* marry Lettie before she expires." She bounced over to Lady Charles. "Mama, Lettie scratched her finger making the kissing bough and we came for some salve."

Across the room, Sylvia and Lady Charles shared an indulgent smile. Naturally, it needed all four of them to fetch the salve. Christmas festivities did have the effect of making people silly, and being in a group was only making the girls sillier.

Dear heaven, Sylvia had been the same age as Prudence Babworth when she and Michael ran hand in hand out of the church in Birmingham, amid their families' cheers and a shower of rice. How worldly and wise she had thought herself, and more than ready to run her own household with her wonderful Michael Ray, with his heady promises of adventure and excitement and wealth.

Well, there had been wealth, until it had disappeared like smoke, after which the adventure and excitement had consisted entirely of evading the consequences of her husband's incessant lies and even more incessant debts.

She doubted anyone had ever called Graham Ossett exciting, but while twenty-year-old Sylvia would have screamed at the idea of dull reliability, she now found reliability to be not remotely dull, not when it was a matter of food reliably on the table and a roof reliably over her head.

The girls were waiting. Smiling, she waved the pages.

"Yes, this letter is from Mr. Ossett. He adores writing to

me," she added, injecting satisfaction into her tone and making them sigh.

She folded the letter twice, and then, perhaps a tad carried away by this image of herself as a desirable and worldly older woman (who had, after all, shocked herself by planting a kiss on a handsome young man today), she slid the folded paper into the bodice of her dress with a wink.

"Is he *very* handsome?" Miss Lettie asked. "Anyone who owns a manor house must be handsome."

"That doesn't stand at all," Emily argued, retrieving the salve from a cabinet. "Is he exciting and adventurous? That's the important part."

Jane gave a resigned sigh. "Emily means to marry a pirate one day."

"Mr. Ossett is no pirate, alas," Sylvia said. "You might find him old, for he's forty." This horrific statistic made Miss Lettie wrinkle her nose. "But as I am just turned three-and-thirty, he's a very good age for me."

"Mr. DeWitt is about seven years older than Prudence," Miss Lettie giggled. "Mr. *Isaac* DeWitt, I mean. Mr. Isaac hasn't a country estate, but he does own a townhouse and Prudence wants to marry him."

"No, I don't. I don't even like him," Prudence flashed back. "Tell us more about your Mr. Ossett, Mrs. Ray. How did you meet him? Was it love at first sight?"

"Mr. Ossett was a customer, interested in some of the cordials I was making and selling in Birmingham. We started talking and—"

"Oh, what did you talk about?"

"You know when conversations just flow?" she prevaricated. "And you and the other person are somehow just in accord?"

No need to tell them their conversations had mostly

flowed around Graham's various ailments. That was, he talked about them, while she suggested treatments, only for him to complain that nothing ever worked. What he really wanted, she suspected, was not a cure but for someone to be as fascinated by his health as he was. She quashed her disloyal thoughts. She harbored no false illusions about Graham, and she was sure he harbored none about her.

Graham might seem self-absorbed, but he had been observant enough to perceive Sylvia's situation and to understand that she needed him more than he needed her. By the time of his proposal, they had tacitly understood how their marriage would work. She would tend to his ailments and sympathize with his complaints and ensure his comfort, and in exchange, she'd never have to worry about food or shelter again.

"Does he... Did he kiss you?" Miss Babworth asked. "What is it like, a kiss?"

The memory darted through her: that pleasurable little jolt from the kiss she had stolen from Mr. Isaac in the woods. A kiss was like—what? An opening of the senses, the first words in a new language, in a conversation between bodies and a new way of connecting with another person. A kiss was like a promise.

"You girls have got kissing fever," Sylvia said briskly. "The idea of these kissing boughs has gone to your heads like sherry and you're not behaving sensibly."

"I don't want to behave sensibly," said Miss Lettie, spreading her arms and spinning in a circle. "It's Christmas time!"

"It's almost time to dress for dinner," Jane Newell said.

"I should like some sherry," Miss Babworth said. "Do you think we can have some sherry?"

"Yes, let's have sherry!" Emily agreed.

Then Lady Charles was herding them to the door, saying, mischievously, "Let's see if I can find you some." She followed the horde of girls out, and Sylvia heard her cry, "You're running like elephants!" as they stampeded, giggling, down the hall.

CHAPTER 5

Alone again, in the warmth of Lady Charles's well-equipped still room, soothed by the familiarity of bunches of herbs and distillation equipment and stained books, Sylvia hummed as she tasted her Christmas punch. She was particularly proud of her special punch, not least because sales of it had helped her survive the past two winters, and she was looking forward to serving it to everyone the following day.

She had shyly suggested it to Lady Charles, wanting to offer a gift as thanks for their hospitality, but wary of disrupting their family traditions. Her friend had welcomed the idea enthusiastically, as had Cassandra, who insisted they would serve it to drink around the Yule log on Christmas Day.

And the recipe was just right, she decided as she set aside her tasting cup; by the next day, the punch would be perfect. Congratulating herself, she skipped across the room and almost knocked into someone entering through the other door.

"Mr. Isaac!" she exclaimed.

"Mrs. Ray!"

They froze, staring at each other as if they had completely forgotten how to interact with another human being.

It was Mr. Isaac who remembered himself first. "My apologies. I thought you went out with the other ladies."

"You were there the whole time?"

"I was lurking outside the other door. I didn't wish to… That's to say, it sounded like women's conversation."

Embarrassment fluttered about them like snowflakes at the understanding he had been avoiding her and the reason why. Because she was not safe after all. It had been young Miss Babworth whose kisses he had wanted, yet widowed Mrs. Ray who had forced him to tolerate her kiss.

Looking anywhere but at his face, she noticed he was using a walking stick.

"Your old injury is still bothering you," she said, without thinking. "All that nonsense of climbing trees and tossing women over your shoulder?"

His lips twitched once, twice, and then, oh thank heavens, his face split into that broad smile that she found so ridiculously dazzling.

"Climbing up the tree was easy," he said. "Jumping down from the tree caused the trouble. And the woman in question was easy enough to pick up and whirl around despite her excessive complaints."

She couldn't help smiling back at him. It had not been terrible, hanging over his shoulder, not really. Her legs could still remember the feeling of his arm clamped around them, and her palms mischievously recalled the sensations of his back.

"I suppose the cold doesn't help either," she said. "What was the injury?"

"Broke it, back when I was in the Navy. It was slow

healing at first, but after a summer of daily swimming, it improved well enough. The cold though…" He shook his head. "Always thought it was just an old wives' tale, feeling the cold in your bones. Ten pounds says it'll snow tonight."

"Your leg told you that?

"Actually, the grooms told me that, but I'm sure my leg agrees."

An awkward silence fell, during which they regarded the head of his walking stick, then he waved that stick at a cabinet and headed for it.

"Lady Charles buys in some salve for me. Mine has run out so I came to see if she has more."

"Heat will help," she volunteered, "but you must already know that."

"Yes. The kitchen is heating some sand for me. A bag of hot sand, some salve, an hour's rest, and a good brandy, and I'll be right as rain." He held up a pot from the cabinet. "Mrs. Flores's All-Purpose Balm. Like magic, this stuff."

"Mrs. Flores's medicines are wonderful."

He tossed it up and down like a cricket ball, as he crossed back to her. "You know a lot about it, salves and distillation and so forth."

She watched him approach, letting herself enjoy the sight of him, despite her shame over her wanton, unwanted kiss.

"My father's a physician, and he partnered with an excellent apothecary next door. I found it fascinating, and both were patient with my questions. And what I didn't learn from them, I learned from my mother, who put me to work in her still room from a young age—and very happy I was there too." She nodded at the pot of balm in his hand. "And you know the benefit will be greater if someone else massages it in for you. It's a curious thing, but my father always insisted that another person's hand can achieve a strength and angle one cannot get oneself."

"Is that so?" He flicked a glance at her hands. "I wonder if there's anyone here willing to massage my leg?"

His gaze met hers, that dark, glinting gaze. Her lips fairly tingled with the memory of his.

"You're flirting with me again, Mr. Isaac," she said sternly. "Which I suppose means you still think I'm safe. Even after I—you know."

A little silence pulsed around them.

"I did," he said abruptly. "I do."

"Think I'm safe?"

"Want it. I mean, I didn't mind it."

Another glance: this time at her mouth. She caught herself swiping her tongue over her lower lip; her mouth felt very dry.

Then once more he met her eyes boldly. His air of experience was feigned; his air of confidence was not.

"You said it wasn't pleasant to be kissed by someone when one didn't want it," he explained softly. "But I found it very pleasant. I did want to be kissed. I still do. You merely took me by surprise." A slow smile spread over his face. "A very pleasant surprise."

She huffed away the sly delight blossoming inside her. He was not for her. Those days were gone for her.

"You need not be kind to me," she said. "Those ladies you admire, they're young, but I'm not, and perhaps you might have opinions about widows who make a bit too merry, especially a widow who is engaged to someone else. I'm older than you, seven years or so it seems, and on the wrong side of thirty, and it was quite unacceptable for me to—" She waved a hand. "Do that to you, simply because you pricked my vanity by calling me safe. But there I was, with a handsome young man telling me that he doesn't see me as someone he might ever kiss, and so I suppose I just—"

He kissed her.

It was a soft, swooping kiss. His hand feathered over her cheek, firm and warm, while his mouth brushed hers. The kiss was fast and light and over quickly, though the sensations rippling down her middle were slower to pass.

He paused, his eyes open and intent, his lips hovering over hers, and she lingered too, taken by surprise but liking it—oh, she liked it very much!—his fingers on her cheek, his closeness, his engulfing scent of the pine he had gathered that day.

Once more, desire, so long dormant it was nearly forgotten, curled temptingly between her thighs, so very thrilling and so very, very wrong. But still she let her eyelids flutter closed: an invitation.

It was an invitation he understood. Once more, his mouth moved over hers.

He took his time with this kiss, not quite confident, but not tentative either. His kiss was curious, exploratory. He required neither skill nor experience to send sensations dancing through her. This was her first real kiss in years, and it felt nice.

Very nice.

After he pulled back, he brushed his thumb over her lips as if to seal in his caress. The corners of his lips quirked up. He looked very young, suddenly.

"You're right," he said. "Kissing isn't difficult at all. And I find you lovely to look at and lovely to be near. I didn't consider for a heartbeat your age or your widowhood."

Then, with a frown, he considered the salve.

"The sand must be heated by now, and I truly must rest

my leg if I'm to make it through the evening. You're being kind to me, Mrs. Ray."

"'Tis not kindness, Mr. Isaac."

He made a little moue. "We may not agree about that, but I think we can agree you're definitely not *safe*."

She couldn't help but smile. "Am I suddenly rendered dangerous, by all this kissing?"

"Not dangerous, but let us say, you're rendered very exciting indeed."

CHAPTER 6

After dinner, the whole party gathered excitedly in the drawing room, and Isaac was amused to see that even Lord Tidcombe and the inventors seemed genuinely invested in which of the two kissing boughs would be named the winner.

Cassandra and Lady Charles were the judges, and they proved to be great diplomats, for they awarded both kissing boughs a prize: one for its creativity and the other for its lushness. Then they lit the candles on the boughs, and Isaac and Joshua pulled the ropes to raise them. They automatically competed to raise theirs fastest and highest, only to be forced to back down when it was pointed out that the boughs needed to be low enough for the gentlemen to pluck a berry after each kiss.

By this time, Isaac was feeling quite contented, what with his successful leg treatment and a fine dinner—not to mention that very excellent kiss—and it proved no bother to linger dutifully under the kissing boughs and brush his lips over the cheek of whichever lady wound up in front of him, which was nearly all of them: from Lady Charles, who gave him a maternal pat on his shoulder, to Emily, who gave him a sisterly poke in the belly, to Miss Babworth, who gave him a shy smile. Mrs. Ray alone avoided the kissing boughs. The other gentlemen got into the spirit of it too, and even Joshua stopped complaining long enough to buss each lady on the cheek and toss a berry across the room, before bounding over to Cassandra and whisking her into an impromptu waltz.

Isaac understood the fuss, now. He had looked at Mrs. Ray then, feeling very bold and pleased with himself, and was delighted when she met his eyes—delighted too by the amused warmth in her gaze. Here was a wonderful and unexpected aspect of the kiss: the delicious intimacy of a shared secret.

Next, they passed a merry hour caroling, crowded around the pianoforte to sing together, until the girls declared they wanted to play a game, namely, Bullet Pudding. They were promptly furnished with a large bowl of flour with a bullet placed on top of it. Unsurprisingly, only the young ladies wished to join the game. Bullet Pudding involved scooping out spoonfuls of flour without causing the bullet to fall; whoever did cause the bullet to fall had to dig it out of the flour with their teeth, and only the young ladies saw the appeal in getting a face covered with flour. Tidcombe and the inventors set up a card table, Isaac joined Joshua and Cassandra in playing with little Charlie, and Mrs. Ray chatted with Lady Charles. But when Rose became restive and Lady Charles volunteered to take her back to the nursery, Isaac seized the opportunity, along with a pack of spillikins, to join Mrs. Ray.

"A game of spillikins?" he offered. "You are too sensible to risk digging a bullet out of flour with your teeth, but are you too sensible for this?"

Her smile was warm and welcoming. "I think I've already proven myself to be not sensible today."

"And we are all very grateful."

He dropped onto the chair and took his time releasing the spillikins, letting the carved wooden sticks fall into a haphazard pile of sharp ends.

Mrs. Ray watched, still smiling. "I had forgotten how wonderful Christmas can be," she said. "The coldest, darkest days of the year, and here we are, warm, safe, and well fed, in good company, and enjoying carols and candles and…"

She sighed and sipped her sherry. Would he taste that sherry if he kissed her again now?

"And kisses," he finished for her, softly. "Although I note you don't linger under the mistletoe."

"In my recent experience, mistletoe is not a necessary requirement to get a kiss."

"Interesting. My recent experience is that there are kisses under the mistletoe and kisses in private, and the latter are far superior to the former."

Faint color touched her cheeks. He gestured at the pile, inviting her to go first. She set down her glass and successfully slid out a single spillikin without disturbing the rest.

"Have you come here to play spillikins or to embarrass me?" she asked, as she put it to one side.

"I have come here to flirt with you. But you don't like me flirting with you, so you said."

"I find I don't object so much after all. It makes me feel young, to receive such attention."

Her steady hands chose and safely removed another stick.

"I suspect you're used to looking after people, and used

to doing things for yourself," Isaac said. "And you're being very patient, to suffer my incompetent kiss."

"I didn't suffer, and it wasn't incompetent."

"But, alas, neither did you swoon in bliss at my feet." He grinned. "I suppose I need more practice."

"The recommended way to improve any skill."

She selected another spillikin, but in pulling it out, others shifted. She surrendered the pile to him.

"I learned with my husband," she volunteered, as he successfully slid out a stick and reached for another. "Whatever else I might say of Michael, that aspect of our marriage was highly satisfactory. When you find a woman you want to marry, you can kiss her. You can learn together."

His hand jerked. The spillikins shifted. He cursed.

"But what if... What if I'm no good?" He scowled at the pile of sticks. "What if she dislikes my touch? What if I repel her and she just has to tolerate it? We'd be married and that would be it, forever. By my age, I should know. Shouldn't I? Other men seem to know. Did your husband...?" Shaking his head, he lined up the sticks he had won. "Forgive me. That's too personal. Besides, it's my burden, not yours. Men talk, of course, but that's not conversation I enjoy. Not conversation where I can admit..."

He cleared his throat, embarrassment sweeping over him. But Mrs. Ray's attention was on the spillikins and the game, and that made it easier to talk.

"It was odd, returning to polite society," he said. "Being in the Navy since I was ten—I guess that's why I never got a grasp on the unspoken rules of ladies, the things one does and does not say." He chuckled. "Certainly, I've never had as intimate a conversation with a woman as we're having now."

"A day of firsts for you, then."

"Yes. An excellent day all round."

She flashed him a look and concentrated on easing another spillikin from the pile. Sweet saints, but he appreciated her frankness, and her boldness. Although perhaps boldness was not the right word; rather, she displayed a refusal to be daunted by the sorts of things that did not matter in the end.

Isaac had only been in one really severe shipwreck, the sort that claimed lives, the sort with confusion and chaos and a mouth swollen from saltwater and limbs exhausted from just trying to hold on and survive the relentless waves, the sort that revisited him sometimes, in the night. Some sailors became scared of the sea after such experiences, but others became bolder, because they had already survived the worst. He had been the latter sort; he sensed Sylvia Ray might also be like that.

"I think not every part of your marriage was satisfactory," he said quietly. "I think maybe your late husband did not look after you as well as he should have."

She stiffened, the air about her suddenly as prickly as the spillikins themselves. Conversations were like a game of spillikins, he thought: One never knew when one might pull the wrong stick and cause the whole lot to collapse. This was very useful in an investigation, but perhaps not advisable in a drawing room.

"You're making a lot of assumptions, Mr. Isaac," she said coolly.

"Please don't bother with the 'mister'. Out in the world, I am Mr. DeWitt, but in my brother's house, where there is a surfeit of Misters DeWitt, I'm younger, so he stays Mr. DeWitt and I become Mr. Isaac again, and it makes me feel ten years old."

"Regardless of the use of 'mister,' you still make assumptions."

"Are my assumptions about the late Mr. Ray so wrong, though?" he persisted, despite her chilly tone. "Your husband has been dead a few years, and my guess is you have struggled for at least that long."

She sat straight and silent, staring at the pile of sticks.

This is not an interrogation, Isaac admonished himself. Her previous marriage was not one of the cases of industrial espionage or arson or insurance fraud that he was building his investigative business upon.

Yet still he charged on.

"You've spoken of the unreliability of men and your aversion to certain sorts of men. You seem accustomed to fending for yourself. You have eked out a living using your distillation skills. And Henry Ray has the means to help you, but he has let his son's widow struggle." He paused. She said nothing. "I only met him once, but I recall someone offered him their condolences on his son's death and he said, 'Poor boy. He was undone by that bloody woman.' Are you that woman?"

The knuckles of her clasped hands were white. "Indeed, such marvelous powers of observation and deduction."

"Clues lie everywhere, if one chooses to see. For example, just now, you attributed your enjoyment of this Christmas Eve to feeling safe and warm and well-fed, so perhaps you've not experienced those feelings in some time. Yet your father is a physician and your father-in-law a solicitor, and your education and manner suggest you were not poor as a child." He studied her. "My guess is your husband was a gambler, or something like it."

Her mouth was tight; her dented chin was stiff. He had touched on the truth, or very near to it, and she was ashamed of whatever her husband had done. Earlier, he had overheard her saying that her betrothed owned a manor house, which must be a relief, if her first husband had left her in poverty.

But despite her engagement, she had kissed Isaac today, and welcomed his kiss in return; whatever she felt for her future husband, it was not passion or abiding love. Yes, clues lay everywhere.

"Here's something else I have learned through investigating," he went on. "When I'm getting close to the truth in questioning someone, they become more prickly. You, my dear Mrs. Ray, have become as sharp as this pile of spillikins."

"You did that too." She looked up. "You were very hostile in the woods today. When I uncovered your secret."

Cheers and claps burst out across the room. They both turned. Jane Newell's face was covered in flour, and she gripped the bullet between her teeth. Lady Charles was sitting with Cassandra and Joshua; Isaac had not even noticed her return.

"So perhaps I shall play at this investigation game too," Mrs. Ray said abruptly, a challenge in her blue-green eyes.

She set her elbows on the table and rested her chin on her folded hands to study him. "You joined the Navy when you were ten, which strikes me as very young, but every ship needs a boy and such is the way these things are done. Your father is an earl, and a notoriously bigamous one, and when his bigamy was discovered, you and your brothers were changed overnight from aristocratic heirs to penniless bastards. All this I know because Lady Charles explained a little of the history of how her daughter Cassandra came to marry your brother Joshua, whose name and manufactories are well known in Birmingham." She paused, considering. "I didn't know why you left the Navy until you explained your injury today, so I suspect they considered you to be of no more use." A faint smile touched her lips. "Though if the admirals had seen you climbing that tree today, they might have reconsidered."

He leaned forward. "Was I *very* impressive?"

"Don't come to me for flattery; there are girls enough for that."

She tilted her head, and he thought of her in the woods, reminiscent of a woodland creature. A busy, clever squirrel, perhaps. Better not say that; a lady might not find the comparison flattering.

"I know nothing of how an earl's son might live," she continued, "except what one reads in the papers, but my guess is that, had you grown up as the son of an earl, you might have been kissing women from the age of sixteen or even before."

Isaac shifted, seeing where she was going, discomfort stirring.

"But instead of being a gentleman who could practice kissing, you were living on a ship, and ships, as we all know, don't permit women because sailors are a notoriously superstitious lot and consider women to be bad luck. Yet sailors are also notorious for compensating for the lack of women on their ships by visiting women in every port. Somehow, you missed that part, and did not visit women in ports." She paused, then added, pointedly, "Indeed, I'll guess you've never visited a woman anywhere."

CHAPTER 7

Heat crept over Isaac's neck. This was a terribly intimate conversation, and in her challenge, Mrs. Ray had not hesitated to expose his embarrassing truth: He had never been with a woman.

Yet he could not resent her frankness; he welcomed it.

He tried to ease his embarrassment by tugging at a spillikin, but he was rushed and unsteady and the pile shifted gleefully.

How odd, to sit here in this warm drawing room, with candles glowing, amid friends playing games, and speak of things such as this.

"How are my powers of observation and deduction?" she asked. "Are you *very* impressed by my investigative skills?"

He had to smile. "I'm more impressed by the way you have turned the tables. I exposed something private in your past, so you have exposed something private about me."

"Do you want to stop?"

He considered. He was uncomfortable, very uncomfortable, and it could only get worse, but who knew where it might lead? He did not want to put an end to this —this *revelation* of a conversation.

"I started it," he said. "Take your revenge."

"You don't shy away from uncomfortable situations, then."

"In my experience, staying in an uncomfortable situation is the only way to make it less uncomfortable."

She studied him a moment longer, then focused on sliding a spillikin out. They had lost track of whose turn it was, but the game now was nothing more than something to do with their hands, somewhere to rest their attention when it was too confronting to look at each other.

Another cheer went up from the girls. Again the bullet had fallen, and it was Emily with flour on her face.

"Yet how has this happened?" Mrs. Ray went on. "When sailors get shore leave, they don't sit in churches and crochet blankets for the poor. Surely a young sailor is dragged off to a brothel by older sailors to learn the ways of the world. Yes?" He nodded. She frowned, considering. "Yet somehow, that experience did not take. Why not? Let us guess that perhaps young Isaac witnessed something that made him feel uncomfortable, or perhaps even bad. So when the young sailor is taken to a brothel by older sailors, he is confused about what he wants—am I on the right track?"

He nodded and focused on retrieving a spillikin.

"How old were you when you were first dragged into a brothel? Old enough to have experienced lust, but young enough to be impressionable. Young, I suspect, fourteen or fifteen?"

"Fifteen." His cheeks were flaming. He swiped a hand over his face, then sipped his drink. "This is a very frank conversation."

She was studying him, her expression gentle now. "Am

I right? Did you witness something unpleasant before that, when you were only a boy?" He managed a stiff nod. "Was it very terrible, what you witnessed?"

"Yes. No. I don't know. I was too young to understand, I think. She agreed on the price and the act, but it made me wonder how much choice she truly had. I don't think it was easy for her to bear. And the men, they didn't treat her gently."

"The men."

"Yes."

Silence washed around them, until she continued.

"And a few years later, at fifteen, you found yourself in a small room with a woman... In truth, while a brothel owner was among my customers in Birmingham, I have no knowledge of the inside of a brothel or the lives of the women there, but perhaps the woman you visited didn't seem to be enjoying herself either, so you were reluctant to touch her. But you couldn't admit to the older sailors that nothing had happened, so you lied, claimed experience, and mimicked their way of talking. Over time, you kept lying and avoiding and pretending, and then you were back on land, adjusting to civilian life, and you had no experience and too much pride to admit it." She made a breathy sound of wry amusement. "As you said, clues lie everywhere. The first concern you expressed was that your wife would dislike your touch, that you couldn't bear it if she was repelled by you. Is that why you worked yourself into such a state about a kiss? You're worried about the marriage bed, and your wife not wanting you."

He peered into his empty glass, which remained stubbornly empty. "A very, very frank conversation," he muttered.

"Consider it practice, for when you marry. 'Tis as well to be frank and honest and open with your wife."

"Can I surmise that was another way in which your late husband let you down?"

With a sad smile, she shook her head. He replenished their glasses, grateful for the minor reprieve and the opportunity to let the subject rest.

"Is it so very long since you enjoyed Christmas?" he asked, as she sipped her fresh sherry.

"Our first few Christmases as a married couple were very enjoyable. I loved decorating my own house. By our fourth Christmas, we hadn't enough money for pudding and goose, so we spent it with my family, though we didn't explain why. The fifth Christmas we spent with my husband's family, and never told anyone we had moved to rented rooms. The sixth Christmas, he was in debtors' prison."

"That can't have been easy for you."

"At least then I knew where he was." She sighed. "I've always hated the idea of debtors' prison. The very concept seems so absurd and cruel, for how is one to pay debts from a cell? They hold a man ransom for his family to pay. But I confess I was a little relieved. At least, I thought, he can't get into more debt there."

She followed this with a short, bitter laugh.

"Michael was very charming, very persuasive," she went on. "Not a gambler, as such, but the sort of man who could sell coal to Newcastle, as they say. He made a fortune selling investments on the promise of astounding dividends that never arrived, which upset his investors quite a bit. But he always had another scheme in mind, and then another. He was so persuasive, so believable—I think because he himself truly believed that each of his schemes would make him and everyone else rich. And even in debtors' prison…"

"Oh no. Let me guess." Isaac leaned forward. "He made more promises of great wealth while in prison?"

"To the warden, no less. The warden was so excited by his scheme, he fiddled the books to release him early, gathered money from his friends, and handed it all over to Michael."

Isaac tried to stifle his laughter. "I'm sorry, it's not funny," he said. "But to persuade the warden! Did he ever pay him back?"

"Of course not." Mrs. Ray's mouth twitched. "I assure you, his next stay in debtors' prison was not nearly so comfortable."

Then she laughed too, so hard she was wiping tears from her eyes, and others in the room were turning to look. She calmed herself with a sip of sherry and a shake of her head.

"Oh, but it *is* funny," she said. "Perhaps not *that* funny, but it feels good to laugh at it finally."

"Forgive me, but there's a piece of the puzzle I don't understand," Isaac said. "Why do you carry the shame for your husband's actions? Why did your father-in-law leave you in poverty?"

"It turned out that Michael was telling his parents I was the reason for his troubles. He claimed I was nagging him for more clothes and jewels and luxuries, and he was only attempting to meet my demands. Yet he was the one who wanted those things; he believed he needed the trappings of material wealth to prove his worth to the world. I *was* nagging him, though. Telling him to stop his nonsense, get a proper job, live frugally until we resolved everything, and him insisting that no, no, this time it would work and why couldn't I have more faith in him? Yet I was scorned and shunned."

"They believed him?"

"It's odd, isn't it, what we'll believe when it serves our interests to do so? They preferred to think ill of me than of him." She set about gathering up the spillikins. "Michael took money from his parents' friends, and my parents and their friends too. Our fathers argued, because Papa would not hear ill of me, and Mr. Ray would not hear ill of Michael. They'd been friends since they were boys, but they nearly came to blows and never spoke again. I think that's partly why my parents moved to Canada. Michael's lies poisoned everyone against me, and my parents' friends shunned them, and their life in Birmingham became intolerable."

"So when your husband died…"

"When my husband died…" She released the spillikins into a haphazard pile on the table. "He left me nothing but debts. Mr. Ray paid off those debts, which was generous of him, and he also paid my rent for a set of rooms for a year, on condition I never contact him again. Mama had left me her distillation equipment, and I made enough money from making and selling cordials to get by. Just."

"So you've learned to do things yourself. For example, you prefer to pick your own mistletoe, rather than rely on a man."

She shook her head, amusement dancing in her eyes. "Foolish. It turns out there are some things one cannot achieve by oneself. An example: trying to pick mistletoe from a tall tree when one is not tall."

"Another example: kissing," he said with a grin, and was delighted when she smiled right back.

CHAPTER 8

The snowfall did begin that night, Sylvia noticed as she readied for bed, just as Mr. Isaac's leg had forecast.

Isaac, rather; no "mister" required.

What an extraordinary conversation that had been. Frank indeed, yet it had released some long-pent-up tension inside her. What a surprising relief to laugh at her troubles with Michael, and somehow, in the telling and the laughing, to let those troubles go.

A hot brick warmed the bed, but Sylvia felt too restless to climb under the blankets just yet. She fizzed with the sort of eagerness she used to feel before a ball or an outing —the anticipation that something delightful was sure to happen. It was one of those wonderful feelings that years of constant struggle had stolen away, without her even noticing, which made feeling it now bittersweet too.

Not a feeling to squander, she decided, so she pulled on her coat and hat, took a lantern, and left her room.

Sunne Park was a curious hodgepodge of styles, having been built first in Tudor times and then added to over the centuries since. At the end of her hallway was a parlor, which led onto a small rooftop area; Sylvia went out there most mornings to greet the day, and it seemed the perfect place to greet the snow. She placed the lantern in a protected nook, then spread her palms and turned up her face to savor the light kisses of the swirling snowflakes.

A sound startled her. She jumped at a figure in the shadows.

"Mrs. Ray, is that you?"

"Mr. Isaac," she said with relief.

"Forgive me for startling you. I came out to look at the snow."

"We had the same idea."

"Would you rather be alone?"

"I'd be glad of company."

Of course. They both had chambers in this wing. She hadn't given any thought to the location of Isaac's room till now.

Side by side, they silently watched the snow swirling in the golden light cast by their lanterns.

"I've seen many marvelous things in this world," he said in a hushed voice, "yet still there's something magical about snow."

"Perhaps because when we were children we found it exciting, and that childish feeling comes back at times like this."

She studied the shadows of his profile: firm jaw, shapely lips, bold nose. He wore no hat, and the snow settled delicately on his dark hair.

She shivered and hugged herself.

"You're cold?" he asked.

"Only a little."

"It would be bold of me to put my arms around you, but perhaps it would keep you warm."

"How bold are you feeling?"

"Maybe not bold enough. But I would like to be bold. With you." He turned his whole body toward her. She turned to him too. He rested a warm hand on one of her shoulders and edged nearer.

"May I... May I kiss you again?" he asked. "I think... Well, I think I liked it."

"You *think*?"

His grin flashed in the night. "It was all so sudden, you see. It would be good to know for sure. I can still feel your kiss on my lips. I keep thinking about it. In truth, I hoped coming out into the snow would cool me down, yet here you are." He paused. "Have I said too much again?"

"No," she said honestly, for she reveled in his confessions, ever since his first confession in the woods, when his anxiety about kissing poured out of him like a river after the rain.

A soft laugh burst out of her, born of simple joy and pleasure in this man. This was precisely why flirtations were dangerous, but surely she was sensible enough to avoid being swept away.

"What's so amusing?" he asked.

"You are being very polite. It's lovely." She smiled at the swirling snow. "And you may, yes."

"Ought I not ask? Should I just grab you and kiss you?"

Before she could reply, he did just that: hauled her into his arms and bent her back. She shrieked with laughter, and he laughed too; they were still half laughing when their mouths met. Their laughter faded as they caressed each other's lips, then she held his face and gently touched her tongue to his. A fresh spiral of pleasure whirled through her. He tensed, but she waited, and a heartbeat later he mimicked her actions, trying it out for himself.

He was, she decided as they parted, a very fast learner.

"Is it like that for you?" he asked.

"Like what?"

"When you kissed me like that, I felt it in my ... um."

She tried not to laugh. "Yes. If it's a good kiss, I definitely feel it in my um."

With a quiet chuckle, he wrapped his arms around her, pulling her into the shelter of his chest and coat.

"I found your mouth," he said, in the tones of a bragging boy. "In the dark. And I didn't break your nose or give you a concussion. I'm making excellent progress."

"You have a natural talent."

"I have an excellent teacher. Though I cannot help but think I'm benefiting more than you are."

"I assure you, I'm enjoying myself very much."

And she was. How good it felt to be wrapped in his warmth. To revel, for these few minutes at least, in the magical excitement of snow and festivities, with an attractive man and secret kisses in the dark. To forget, if only a moment, the struggles that lay behind her, and the dull, dutiful drudgery that lay ahead.

"Mrs. Ray——" he started.

"I think perhaps you can call me Sylvia," she said dryly.

"Sylvia," he repeated, as though testing the shape of her name on his tongue. "I'm trying to be... I understand there are things one does not say or do to a lady, and I'm not always sure where the line is, between what is offensive and what is acceptable."

"I like that you're so honest. It makes you feel safe."

The word was out before she could stop it, but it did not seem to offend him as it had done with her.

"I could kiss you all night, but I'm not sure where to

put my hands or..." He released her then and stepped away. "Sorry. I should go back to my room. Good night."

"Good night."

She watched his silhouette as he picked up his lantern. At the door, he paused and said, in a voice as warm as his kisses, "Merry Christmas, Sylvia."

CHAPTER 9

S ylvia sat in church on Christmas morning and tried very, very hard to listen to the sermon. The pew was cold and hard under her bottom, but her hands were warm in a borrowed muff. Instead of listening, she was thinking about how lovely the countryside had looked this morning under its flawless blanket of snow. She was thinking about her empty stomach and hoping it didn't embarrass her by growling, and she was thinking there was a certain pleasure in being hungry when one knew there was shortly to be a feast.

But mostly she was thinking about Isaac DeWitt, who sat further along the pew from her, on the other side of Lady Charles.

He had greeted her that morning with easygoing cheer, a bold look, and a hint of uncertainty. The combination was beguiling.

I'm not sure where to put my hands, he had said the night before.

You can put them everywhere, she had thought, snuggled up in her warm bed, still fizzing from his touch and the sheer magic of kissing a tempting man amid the first snowfall on Christmas Eve. *You can put your hands wherever you please.*

The feelings were so delicious she indulged them during the return from church, during the Christmas feast of goose and ham—and especially when Isaac raised his glass to her in a silent toast over the spicy, steamy plum pudding. She was keenly aware of him when the party crowded around the fireplace to watch Joshua DeWitt toss on the Yule log, oohing and aahing as the flames burned green. She was aware of him as she served her special Christmas punch, her cheeks glowing from everyone's praise, while their cheeks glowed from her punch.

This bubbling excitement— It was as if the young ladies' merriment had infected her, turning her young too. She was infatuated, and she knew it, and she couldn't help but laugh at herself.

Foolish infatuation, indeed! Foolish, weak, and wicked creature that she was! But it was only for now, she thought; it was only for Christmas, only a few kisses, with a man she would likely never see again once she left this place. None of it felt quite real anyway, as if Lady Charles's invitation had plucked her out of her real life and dropped her into a dream.

So she made no objection to be seated close to Isaac when the entire party huddled around a bowl of brandy-soaked raisins for the traditional Christmas game of Snapdragon. Neither did she object when his leg bumped against hers. He mumbled a hasty apology. She smiled her forgiveness.

All the candles were extinguished but for those on the kissing boughs, and Mr. DeWitt, with a flourish and a wink, set fire to the raisins. Blue flames danced over the bowl. In the eerie light, everyone laughed at each other's faces, blue and ghostly and shadowed. Isaac met her eyes and grinned, ghoulish in that flickering blue glow, and she wondered if she dared let her leg fall against his. She did not, though she was aware of every inch of him and wondered if he was just as aware of her, even while he exchanged quips with Miss Babworth and Emily.

Mr. DeWitt insisted that his wife be the first to play: to snatch a raisin from the flames without getting singed. Cassandra grabbed a raisin triumphantly and discovered she had, on her first go, taken one of the many raisins into which a button had been pressed, thus earning a boon.

"What will be your boon, Cassandra?" Emily asked. "What will you demand, and of whom will you demand it?"

Her husband leaned back in his chair and grinned broadly. "Yes, Cassandra, my love, what will you demand? Do make a demand of me. I adore it when you make demands of me."

Cassandra slipped a hand onto his shoulder, as she considered the group thoughtfully. Her gaze rested on Sylvia. "I demand that Mrs. Ray gives me the recipe for her special Christmas punch."

The turn passed to Emily, who squealed as she stole a raisin from the flames. Down the table, Joshua DeWitt leaned close to his wife and Sylvia heard him say, "That's your polite request. What boon do you really want to demand?"

"You behave yourself," she scolded him fondly, which only resulted in an unrepentant grin.

"I am looking forward to behaving myself," he said. "I assure you, Mrs. DeWitt, I shall behave myself all night long."

Their intimacy was palpable, even amid the squealing and the eerie light, and Sylvia shifted on her chair and nervously arranged her skirts. Her hand bumped Isaac's under the table. She went very still. From the corner of her eye, she watched him stare ahead, also tense. Without looking at her, he brushed his hand back and forth against hers, in a tentative but unmistakable caress.

Sylvia kept her eyes on the flames dancing over the brandy-sodden raisins. Without knowing her own intention, she curled her little finger around his. A tiny smile snagged the corner of his lips; she fought her own smile of absurd satisfaction.

If only they could last forever, these winter nights in this drawing room. All the guests were orphans of a sort, she realized; the family had made no plans as Cassandra had delivered her second child only a few months before. There were the Babworth sisters, who lived on the estate, but whose parents had gone away. Each of the male guests was without family, for various reasons, and here was Sylvia too, as Graham had wished to defer their wedding until the new year.

It was just for Christmas, she reminded herself, these magical, not-quite-real weeks in this house, this transitory period between her past as an impoverished widow in Birmingham, and her future as the dutiful wife of a staid gentleman in Worcestershire.

Real life would intrude, as it always did, and she would be responsible and well-behaved and sensible again. But this was not real, and she would enjoy her foolishness and infatuation, for if one thing was certain in this world, it was that she would never have a chance like this again.

"MIGHT I interest you in a game of piquet, Mrs. Ray?"

Isaac had spotted Sylvia sitting alone by the fire, gazing

at the flames in a reverie, and he had scooped up the cards without a second thought.

After the game of Snapdragon, with all the raisins gone, the button boons claimed, and singed fingers and scalded tongues compared and commiserated over, the party settled into more peaceful activities. The girls were singing again, their high spirits mellowed to something more gentle and sweet, and the other men were engaged in a lazy sort of conversation, which Isaac had listened to with half an ear. Lady Charles had retired to bed, and Joshua and Cassandra had excused themselves too.

Mrs. Ray—Sylvia—said, "Thank you, I'd like that."

As they took their seats, their eyes met; he would swear something passed between them. An intoxicating smile played around her lips as she watched him shuffle the cards.

"What's that smile for?" he asked.

She leaned across the table to speak softly. "You, Mr. Isaac DeWitt. You may not have the experience of a rake, but you certainly have the instincts of one."

He paused mid-shuffle, uncertain. "Am I behaving very badly?"

"You must not behave like this with the young ladies."

"Perhaps you bring out my rakishness." He fought a smile. "But do not fear. I'm not a rake, I think, for I'd be very content with a wife, should I ever figure out how to get one."

Sylvia shot a glance at the young women gathered around the pianoforte, studying the sheet music to choose their next song.

"And so Miss Babworth enters the scene," she said.

"Perhaps. Not necessarily Miss Babworth, but someone like her."

As he dealt the cards, his thoughts returned, yet again,

to the empty rooms of his house. He had hoped the house would serve as an anchor in his new life on land, but coming home to its echoing emptiness just left him feeling more alone.

"One of my early investigations proved lucrative, for I located a valuable lost shipment and my reward was a quarter of its worth," he said. "I bought a townhouse, but I did it hastily, and it's too big and empty for me. But I wanted a place. I wanted…"

She picked up her cards and began to sort them. "Shall we play the guessing game again? You spent more than half your life at sea, where you had a clear, defined place, but back on land, you were adrift, if I can say that, and wanted to lay down roots."

He shook his head. "I'm transparent to you, it seems."

She lay down her first card, and they played in silence for a while, until she asked, "Do you know what you seek in a wife?"

He glanced at her, but her eyes were on her cards, and her tone was distracted.

"A partner, I suppose," he replied. "It doesn't sound very romantic, put like that, but I'm building my life anew, and I like the idea of a wife who can build that life with me. My income is sufficient to support a family, but I don't want an ornament, though, to be honest, a decent dowry won't go astray."

He twisted to consider Prudence Babworth, singing at the pianoforte. She looked very pretty, with the firelight gilding her sandy hair and her voice rising with the song, sweet and high and true. She knew how to run a household. She had received a good education and displayed a head for numbers and a practical bent, for all that the Christmas festivities were turning her silly. She was easy enough to talk to. Isaac liked her, though he felt nothing like what others described as love. Romantic love seemed a pointless approach to courtship. Isaac felt no need to wail about flowers and starlight or whatever other nonsense seemed to pass as romantic love, and he didn't feel any the poorer for that.

On balance, Prudence had not seemed like a bad choice.

Yet he had been unable to kiss her. It was easier with Sylvia because she knew things that a virtuous young lady like Prudence could not yet know. Even if he didn't court Miss Babworth, he would want to court someone like her, and this same problem would arise again and again.

Well, at least he could kiss a lady with some confidence now, thanks to Sylvia. *Just talk to your wife,* she had said. *You can learn together.* But what if he couldn't? What if his bride recoiled from his touch? He had heard plenty of men joke about their wives having headaches every night. If such men's jokes were any indication, there were plenty of marriages where women did not want their husbands, and men did not want their wives, yet they had to stay married, because those were the rules. Isaac very much wanted to be wanted, and stay wanted, by his domestic partner in life.

He twisted back. "Do my criteria sound foolish?"

"You've thought about it carefully. It's good to know what you want."

"Are you getting what you want?"

She studied her cards intently. "I'm at a different stage of life than you are, and than they are," she added with a nod at the young ladies. "To think I was the same age as Miss Babworth when I first married and yet… She seems so young."

"And I again I say, you're not what we could call old."

"It's all relative, isn't it? Perhaps I speak not of bodies, but of the spirit. When I was that age, I longed for excitement. Now, I long for security."

"And you'll have it."

He didn't want to ask about the man she would marry. He already knew enough: The man was older than she was, and he owned a country estate.

She sighed. "I didn't spare him a thought when I was kissing you. That's a shameful thing to confess."

"I don't wish to make you feel ashamed."

"You haven't. I feel even guiltier because I don't feel ashamed. I didn't know this about myself. It seems I have a touch of the wanton in me. Do I repel you for that?"

"Not at all. I'm happy for a touch of the wanton." She groaned at his terrible joke. Encouraged, he added, "Now, if you're a wanton and I'm a rake, we'll rub along well together." He froze. Maybe that took the joke too far. "By 'rub,' I mean…" he stammered. "I don't mean… That isn't to say…"

She only laughed. "We're getting very risqué over in this corner of the room."

"Quick, play your cards so no one will guess."

She slapped down a card, then he slapped one down too, and then they were both slapping down cards, trying not to laugh, and neither of them paying the least bit of attention to the game.

"It's a revelation," he said. "All these new experiences. Kissing is not just kissing, it's…"

It meant shared looks, secret touches. It meant frank conversations and a thrilling mix of feeling both comfortable and nervous. Nervous in the good way, the anticipatory way.

"Anyway, I appreciate it," he finished weakly.

She raised her eyebrows in question.

"You," he said. "I'm being clumsy, in word and deed,

but I'm grateful to you, I mean, for tolerating my fumbling incompetence while I'm reveling in these new experiences."

"You're charming and you know it. And not at all incompetent. I enjoyed it yesterday. Very much. More than I ought to."

"I did too."

She flicked the corner of her cards with one neat, mesmerizing finger, again and again. He had touched that hand under the table. He had kissed those lips. And he had tossed and turned in his bed, thinking about it over and over again. About what lay under her clothes and how her body would feel under his palms.

She looked up suddenly. "There's more, you know."

He kept his expression solemn. "I had suspected there might be. Other body parts and such."

"Yes. Other experiences."

A faintly troubled look crossed her face. She looked away. She clearly had no great passion for her betrothed, but practical marriages of convenience were more common than not.

He reconsidered what she had said, about what it meant to be young.

"I don't believe that growing older means never again experiencing excitement or pleasure," he said slowly. "You said when you were young, you craved excitement and now you want security. But must security be dull? Are you never to know excitement again?"

"I don't know." Sadness shadowed her tone.

In the silence, he gathered up the cards and shuffled them. He watched her watching his hands. She bit her lip. He wanted to bite it too, he thought, wickedly. And her neck, there.

Desire bolted through him.

Her eyes snapped up to meet his. He blinked, hoping his thoughts had not shown on his face.

"I could show you," she said. "If you wanted."

His hands stilled. She swallowed nervously, and her cheeks pinked, but she held his gaze. His breath felt shorter; his chest felt tight. Was that a proposition? He wasn't sure. What if he had misunderstood?

"You said last night I'm a good teacher, and I know it was only a jest but..." She studied her fingers, tangling with each other on the table. "In a couple of weeks, I'll leave here, rather plumper than when I arrived, happily. What I'm going to won't be perfect, but it will be better than what I've left behind. Here, I feel like I'm in some magical in-between land, and my youthful spirit, which I thought long gone, is beginning to stir, and I want..." She shook her head. "Never mind. I don't know what I want."

"You want to feel young again," he said.

She nodded. She called herself "old," but he suspected she actually meant "tired."

"And you think that maybe I could ... make you feel young."

"Maybe you could." Then she straightened and spoke more briskly. "Forgive me, I don't know what possessed me to make a proposition like that."

So it had been a proposition. She was brave to make it, in the circumstances. That courage made him like her even more.

"No need to excuse yourself to me," he said, his mind racing with the possibilities. "I'm grateful you don't judge me, so I'm not about to judge you."

He kept shuffling the pack of cards, absent-mindedly. Her eyes were elsewhere: on the kissing boughs, the pianoforte, the rug, the door. He feared she would leave, and this moment would be lost. He slid his foot against hers. She sat straighter and swiped her tongue across her lips. She did not move her foot away.

Isaac, aware of the others in the room, pitched his voice low, his tone casual, even as his heart pounded and his fingers felt clumsy on the suddenly thick cards.

"Let's be clear, because I don't always understand what women are saying or what they mean. So I want us to be very clear…"

He jerked his hands up, releasing the cards. They flew up into the air, snowed back down over him, over the table, down onto the floor. She gasped in surprise.

But when he bent to pick them up, she did too. Thankful his plan was working, he grabbed her hand to hold her in place.

She frowned, then her face relaxed; he knew she had understood his scheme to steal a moment's privacy under the table.

"Your proposition," he whispered. "You speak of seduction, of…"

She hissed in a sharp breath. He feared she would retreat, but instead she said, in a trembling whisper, "An affair, I might say."

"With kissing and … everything?"

"Everything," she confirmed.

Still Isaac wanted to be sure. "You will show me, teach me … everything."

"And you…" She glanced down at their hands. He reluctantly let her go. "You will give me memories. A little magic to make me feel young and carefree, perhaps for the last time in my life."

He hastily gathered the cards and sat up and continued shuffling. His hands were so unsteady, he feared he'd send them flying again. She very carefully laid the cards she had gathered on the table and stared at them.

"Isaac," she said to the cards. "Say something please. Anything. I hardly recognize myself. I've never said anything so brazen in my life, and I never shall again." She looked up, her eyes wide and uncertain. "What do you say?"

He held her gaze. "I say yes."

CHAPTER 10

The snow crunched under Sylvia's boots and her breath made puffs of cloud in the air, as she headed through the woods to the hunting cabin Isaac had suggested, when Sylvia confessed she didn't feel comfortable meeting in the house.

Two robin redbreasts watched her from a tangle of bare brambles, the only witnesses to her crime.

Slipping away unnoticed had been easy, as it was Boxing Day, and the ladies of the house were visiting tenants and villagers to distribute gifts.

A little whisper in her head had been scolding her all morning, listing the reasons not to do this: She was betrothed; she was virtuous; this was wicked and wrong. Yet her body went about dressing and chatting and concealing one of her sponges in her dress, as if there were no voice in her head at all. With each step along the snowy path, the voice faded to nothing under the rising symphony of her anticipation.

Smoke curled up from the cabin's chimney. Isaac was

already there, just as he'd promised. She pushed open the door with a trembling hand and slipped inside.

It was a small cabin, simple but clean, and warm thanks to the fire crackling merrily in the hearth. Candles burned on the table, on which Isaac was setting out some wine and a small plate of mince pies.

He spun around, looking as guilty as a thief. But when their eyes met, he straightened and his mouth did that thing she enjoyed so much, where a smile twitched, lurked, twitched again, and then burst out. She felt that smile, felt his warmth and welcome. Here was a memory to treasure already, she thought. Already it had begun. Already she felt youthful and foolish and carefree.

"You look lovely," he said, raking back his hair with a nervous laugh.

"Thank you."

"I'm glad you came."

"I'm glad you came." She unpinned her hat. "It's wonderfully warm in here. Thank you for thinking of it."

"I want you to be comfortable. I want…" He huffed out. "I'm not sure what to do."

She brushed her fingers over his jaw, taking her time. Every moment would make a memory: *the Christmas I was wicked*.

"I do believe that's why you have a teacher."

"It feels strange, that's all. I'm used to knowing what to do."

"You could begin by helping me take off my coat."

"Yes!" He leaped toward her, only to pause, his hands hovering over the buttons.

"You may touch me," she said softly. "We're not in your sister-in-law's drawing room taking tea with the vicar. I want to be here. With you. Doing this." Her words seemed to relax him. "Besides," she added, "we've already established you have the instincts of a rake. Give them free rein."

"If you'll give your wanton free rein."

"Oh, she's definitely taking the lead over me now. My more virtuous parts are reaching for their smelling salts before they swoon over my scandalous behavior."

On cue, that rakish glint lit his expression. "Surely the first order of duty for any rake is to make a woman forget her virtuous parts even exist. If you're to swoon over anything, my lovely, it should be over me."

"And how might you achieve that?"

"I could begin by greeting you properly," he murmured. He brushed a hand over her cheek, his palm wonderfully warm on her cold skin. Then he lowered his head and gave her a kiss: gentle, thrilling, soft.

"Your kiss…" she whispered.

"Improved?"

"Felt it in my um."

Faint color stained his cheeks.

"Are you *blushing*?" she asked.

"No. Maybe. A little. Yes."

So help her, but how she delighted in this man! She caressed his cheek and earned a yelp.

"Oh hell, your hand's cold, even with the gloves," he said. "Terrible for you to be cold."

He tugged off her gloves, taking the time to rub her cold hands between his warm ones. He planted kisses on her palms, and then on her wrists, and then he paused, studying her arms with a frown.

"Is something wrong?" she murmured. "They are typical sorts of arm, I'm assured."

"Nothing. I'm simply … getting a sense of possibilities." Perhaps her confusion showed in her face, for he added, "It occurs to me there's a lot of you to discover. I mean, *arms.*" He gulped in apparent amazement, like a pauper before a feast. "How wonderful are arms? Very wonderful. And then there are hands and wrists and elbows and shoulders and— Let's see about this coat." He widened his eyes with playful excitement. "Who knows what wonders lie under this here coat? What do you think I'll find?"

"I don't know. Best be careful. Could be bears."

The coat undone, he pushed it off her shoulders and went to hang it up. That was a lovely surprise, but she said nothing. Better not make him self-conscious again. Besides, if she was training him to be a good husband, then his future wife would thank her for endorsing his good habits.

No: Do not think of his future wife. Or her future husband.

She launched herself at him to dispel those thoughts. What was inside this cabin was all that mattered right now. This was her interlude. Her fantasy holiday from the practicalities of her real life.

"We didn't talk about…" he started. "Babies, I mean."

"Thank you for asking, but I'm taking care of it." She wasn't even sure if she could have children, but now was not the time to speak of that. "Now, you take care of my dress."

She turned her back on him, to show him the fastening of her gown. It was one of her older gowns, but it was in good enough condition and she had reworked it to give it some semblance of fashionability. She'd not worn it in years, for wearing it needed a maid's help, and maids hadn't been part of her life for some time. Besides, she had been too thin and it had hung off her, but her gorgeous gluttony this past fortnight had redressed that.

"If I'd realized how much time would be required to get you out of your clothes, I'd have allowed an extra three hours," he grumbled, as he attacked the fastenings, his fingers warm and gentle as they bumped against her spine.

"Navigating the complexities of a woman's clothing is probably the most difficult aspect of this entire venture," she warned him. "If you master this part of the lesson, the rest is smooth sailing."

"This cropped up in a Greek legend. Undressing an English lady was one of the impossible labors of Hercules, I believe."

"I don't remember that one."

"Oh, yes. The tasks included slaying lions, stealing from goddesses, and figuring out how on earth to get an Englishwoman out of her clothes."

She laughed. "If you're in a hurry, we could just toss my skirts over my head."

"Not on your life. A beautiful woman is offering to let me see her naked, and I shall slay any lion that dares try to stop me."

She glanced at him over her shoulder. "And pay attention. You must remember how it's done so you can do it back up again."

"Too hard," he said. "You'll just have to stay naked forever."

He'd undone all the buttons, slid her dress down her body, and unlaced her stays. For a moment, they stood still, not touching, then his knuckles brushed the back of her neck. Erotic thrills shivered through her; she straightened her spine and giggled despite herself. He chuckled, his mouth so close to her shoulder that his breath warmed her skin.

"And necks and spines. *And* you're ticklish," he whispered on a note of awe. "The wonders are never-ending. How are we supposed to... when we... Oh hell."

She leaned back against him. He dropped his head against hers. His breathing was ragged. His heart raced.

"Isaac?" she whispered. "What's wrong?"

"Nothing. I'm torn. I… I want to explore every inch of you, learning what happens when I touch you."

"That sounds lovely."

"But I also have a very pressing need and it's driving me wild, and I'm trying to distract myself by focusing on your buttons and laces and pulleys and winches and everything else that holds your gown together, but Sylvia," he groaned. "I don't know if I can draw this out. I'm feeling very crude right now."

She turned in his arms. "Then it's time to get you out of your clothes. Because I mean to enjoy the sight too."

She tugged his shirt out of his breeches. He caught her hands.

"I don't require lessons in undressing myself," he said. "I learned how to do that some years ago."

"Hush. I'm enjoying myself. Now lift your arms."

He obeyed, but she almost immediately ran into trouble, being, as he mumbled through the linen covering his face, somewhat shorter than he was. Finally, she conceded defeat and told him to remove the shirt himself. He could not have shed the item faster had it been on fire.

He was well muscled, rangy and lean. More loose strands of his hair than usual fell about his face, giving him more of a rakish air. She let her eye roam over him, over his shoulders and chest, his arms and hands, which were moving from position to position, as if he wasn't sure where to put them. She suddenly understood his sense of wonder. There was so much of Isaac DeWitt to discover. A panicky feeling swept over her: A week or so together would never be enough.

Better get started, then.

She rested her hands on his chest, soaking up the feel of hard muscles and smooth, scented skin. He caught his breath, swallowed hard. His tongue swiped over his lips.

"Are you all right? Look at your breeches." She slid her hand down over them, over his hard, thick bulge. "I wonder what's in here," she teased, playing his words back to him. "Whatever will we find, do you think?"

His entire body stiffened. His hands gripped her hips. His eyes were squeezed shut.

"Wait," he gasped. "Don't."

She froze. "Isaac? What's wrong? Talk to me."

He said nothing. She curled her hand around his neck and pulled herself up to feather kisses over his jaw. His arm came around her like a steel band. His fingers dug into her flesh. A strangled groan tore out of him, as his whole body shuddered against hers.

Oh. Oh dear. He had not been able to last. She hadn't thought of that. She had never discussed such things with Michael. She wasn't a good teacher after all.

She held him. To her relief, he kept holding her. Through his ragged breathing, he swore with such fluency and creativity she understood why sailors were renowned for cursing.

"I didn't think," she whispered. "I'm sorry."

A cascade of breaths. "*You're* sorry," he rasped. "I wanted this to be good. For both of us. Now I've ruined everything."

CHAPTER 11

Isaac released Sylvia and dropped down onto the bed, his eyes squeezed shut. He couldn't bear to look at her, to see her disappointment. He still wore his breeches. He supposed he would stay dressed now. What a mess.

Literally.

He heard her moving about. When he dared open his eyes, it was to see her disappear into the next room. He dragged himself up the mattress and slumped back down on the pillows, slinging his forearm over his eyes. Pleasure still pulsed in his useless, worthless, traitorous cock. His body still tingled with delight from her caress and the intoxicating fragrance of her skin. He'd hardly even touched her.

She came back in. He let his senses track her movements. Was she getting dressed to go? But she needed his help to dress. Oh no, sweet saints, would he have to help her dress again now? While he had spilled in his breeches like a boy half his age.

Then the mattress sank under her weight.

"So you've ruined everything, have you?" she asked lightly. "What a tragedy."

He lifted his forearm just enough to see her. His breath stopped. She had removed her underclothing and knelt, naked, beside his knees. Naked, with lovely, round breasts and smooth shoulders and the curves of her stomach and thighs and the promise of the curls between them.

He pressed his hands into the mattress to shove himself upright, not daring to take his eyes off her.

"You're beautiful," he said. "And naked. Very naked. Why did you…" He waved an unsteady hand at her nakedness.

She raised her eyebrows. "Why did I bother to finish undressing when you seem to have finished for the day?"

How to respond to that? Her tone was mild, playful even. She wasn't annoyed, or mocking, or disappointed.

Instead, she smiled, fondly, it seemed. "Because I'm not finished with you, Isaac. Personally, I am exceedingly satisfied with the way matters are proceeding."

"You are?"

"If you were still erect and ravenous, you'd have been so distracted by the demands of your ravening erection, you might have completely ignored me."

He scoffed. "I couldn't be in a room with you and ignore you."

"That's the thing about naked bodies. They do tend to get noticed."

"Not just when you're naked. I always notice you."

"Always the charmer. The flattery isn't necessary."

It wasn't flattery, though. It was true. He hadn't realized until now, but he was always aware of her. That was why he had noticed she had left the group during the expedition to gather greenery; that was why he had found her stuck. But it was not worth arguing the point.

It was not possible to argue the point, either, as she planted a hand on his thigh, giving him some of her weight as she leaned toward him. Her breasts moved. He stared, mesmerized. Breasts. Naked woman. Hand touching him. Breasts!

"You must not feel awkward," she was saying, "for this is an excellent development."

He tried to focus on her words. "How can this be good? I mean, isn't all that—" He waved a hand in the general direction of his groin. "Essential to the whole thing?"

"How like a man to believe nothing can continue without him. There is much more, which I can now teach you without you being distracted by—" She too gestured at his groin. "All that."

"But don't you need me hard for us to…"

He sighed. He wanted to touch her breasts. Maybe this was what she meant. He sat up, spirits renewed. She made an excellent point. His erection, or lack thereof, was not nearly so interesting to him as the thought of those breasts under his hands. And her stomach. And her thighs. And her … um.

"Was that erection unusual for you?" she asked.

Jerked out of his reverie, he blinked at her, stunned by the ridiculousness of the question. "It was unusually intense, if that's what you mean."

"But it was not the first erection you ever experienced?"

She was sounding matter of fact now, like a Navy doctor running through a compulsory examination.

"Of course not," he said.

"And that was not your first climax."

"Um. No."

"And how many do you get in a lifetime?"

"How many?" he repeated, more confused by the second.

"Yes. How many erections and climaxes have been allotted to you for your lifetime? Was that it, then? Have you used them all up?" She sighed dramatically. "Complete quota expended, and the man not yet seven-and-twenty." Her fingers were tracing lazy shapes on his thigh. His blood stirred in response. "Shall we hold a wake? Raise a tombstone to it, perhaps? *'In memory of the final erection of Isaac DeWitt. Alas, let us weep, for never will he cometh again.'*"

He smiled despite himself. "You're teasing me."

Mischief danced in her eyes. "I would like to suggest that maybe, given a little time, you might be able to manage another one. And maybe that was not your last one ever."

He scowled at her. "You don't know that. It might have been. Then you'd be sorry." He straightened. "Wouldn't you?"

"I would be very sorry, and I would dedicate myself assiduously to helping you recover. But I'd like to make two points. First, I don't think you'll need much help recovering. And second, for now, we don't need it, if you don't need me to pander to your wounded self-regard. Now you can dedicate all your attention to me. How does that sound?"

"Would I get to touch your breasts?"

He cringed at his eager tone, but she laughed, a sweet melodic sound of pure pleasure that coursed right through him, curling up in his groin, and whether it was her breasts —Breasts! He'd get to touch them!—or her laughter, he realized she was absolutely right about his imminent recovery.

"I hope you will," she said. "I hope you'll touch a lot

more of me than that. So take off your breeches and let your lesson begin."

"But you don't need—"

"Stop arguing and do as you are told."

"Aye-aye, captain," he said, and hastened to obey.

HERE WAS another thing Isaac had never imagined: the pleasure of having a woman look at his naked body the way Sylvia was looking at him.

But then a shadow crossed her expression. She bit her lip.

"I wish to show you how I experience pleasure," she said, frowning. "Make sure you learn the fundamentals."

"Good. Yes. Let's do that."

"But I've never taught anyone before, and I'm trying to figure out how it should be done. Perhaps... Yes."

He followed her instructions when she ordered him to sit up and part his legs. As she had predicted, he was already recovering nicely from his ordeal. She glanced down at his slight erection.

"It's alive!" she whispered mischievously. "A miracle."

"Must be a miracle worker around here, raising the dead."

To his surprise, she climbed between his legs, treating him to a very welcome view of her backside, and lay against him, her back against his chest. Sensations overwhelmed him: her weight and heat blending with his, the press of her naked buttocks against his increasingly interested cock. The unexpected awkwardness of arranging their limbs. But also— Why?

"What are we doing?" he asked.

"We're teaching you how to pleasure me." He could

hear the sheepish smile in her voice. "But this is the only way I know how to do it, so you'll have to learn from my perspective."

"How very practical you are."

He tentatively placed his hands on her stomach. With a soft sigh, she relaxed back into him. This was good, he thought, very good, grateful she couldn't see his face. He slid his hands up, up, slowly, to her breasts. He cupped them, reveling in their weight and softness and warmth. Oh, sweet saints, but this was good.

"Do you like that?" he murmured. "Am I doing it right?"

She made a little humming sound. "Nice."

"This is what you wanted?"

"It's a start."

She guided one of his hands down over her body. After a hesitation, she lifted one of her legs over his, and his eyes were drawn helplessly downward, to the tableau they made, the rises and valleys of her body, her parted thighs, their tangled legs. His blood was rushing madly now; she must be able to feel it. She rested her head on his shoulder and he dragged his gaze back to her face, to see her closed eyes, her intent expression. Still she guided his hand, guided it onto her warm, silken thigh, guided it upward. An odd noise escaped his throat as their entwined fingers touched her soft, wet heat. She responded with a breathy sigh.

"This?" he murmured. "What you want?"

Hot. Soft. Wet. And— Hell. There was an awful lot more going on down there than sketches had led him to believe. A woman's anatomy was not a simple matter, he realized, craning his head to see her better. Her scent teased him; his body leaped again. They would definitely not need to raise a tombstone to his final erection, given his erection was already raising itself. She must have noticed it, but she ignored him, so he must too.

Somewhere through the waves of sensation washing over him, he heard her voice, like an angel speaking in a dream, as she explained, somewhat haltingly, that women had a place that was very sensitive and a site of much pleasure.

"I've heard tell of it," he said. "Some sailors mentioned it, but others say it doesn't exist."

"They'll believe in mermaids and sea dragons, but not that a woman can experience pleasure. Here."

She pressed his finger into her and rolled her hips between his. Her matter-of-fact manner was perfect, just perfect. He tried to concentrate, but no thought stayed in his head for longer than a heartbeat. Nothing stayed but the feel of her inviting heat, as she showed him how to touch her. Then there were her gasps and moans, the way she wriggled and shivered and shuddered on top of him when he got it right. A reward of sorts: the exquisite, torturous pleasure of her body pressed against his, as her hips rolled and her back quivered. He tentatively caressed one of her breasts with his other hand, plucking at her nipple with his thumb. She arched with pleasure. Fascinating! A faint smile curved her parted lips, her eyes were closed, her expression blissful. He longed to kiss her again, but could not reach.

So instead he obeyed her breathy commands of "there!" and "like that" and "faster now!"

She released his hand—he was steering the ship solo now—and gripped his thighs, her body tense.

"Don't stop," she hissed, and then "yes," she sighed, and then "Oh, dear heaven Isaac, you are…"

Isaac could not wonder what he was, because now he

was wondering if he was about to spend his seed again, just from her body rubbing against his.

But her fingers dug harder into his thighs—the pain provided a welcome distraction—and a strangled cry flew from her throat. First she went very still, and then a shudder rippled through her entire body.

Well. Isaac knew what *that* was.

A grin split his face. His chest swelled as if he had single-handedly sailed a frigate into harbor. He rested his well-exercised hand on her stomach and watched the uneven rise and fall of her lovely breasts.

She slid to one side so she could look up at him.

"That was lovely," she breathed. Her hand roamed cheekily up his thigh, fumbling behind her, finding his eager cock. "It looks like someone has decided to join the dance. Are you ready for your next lesson?"

"Very." He was grinning helplessly, breathing messily. "I am very, very ready to join this dance."

Once more, she took the lead, clambering up to straddle him, giving his very happy eyes an excellent view. Her scent mingled with his in the warm air. He wasn't sure what to do with his hands, so he rested them on her hips.

"Is this when we … um."

She kissed him. "This is definitely when we um."

"Should I…"

"I'll do it this time."

Gently, she guided him to her entrance. Her eyes locked on his and then she slid, slowly, down onto him, her body gripping him, consuming him, *owning* him. Every pleasurable sensation his body had ever felt— He felt everything all at once. The wave of sensation forced his head back, sent a guttural groan pouring out of his throat.

She rose, she sank. Rose, sank. Dazed, Isaac looked everywhere: where they were joined, her soft moving body, the half-smile curving her parted lips, the tenderness in her eyes.

Then she squeezed her muscles around him. He made a strange noise like a winded animal.

He swallowed. "Sylvia?" he croaked.

"I'm right here."

"You're wonderful."

"You are."

He hardly knew what he was doing as he reared up and wrapped his arms around her, and kissed her hard as he thrust up into her.

"I can't," he muttered. "I want."

"I know, sweetheart. Let me go."

CONFUSION CLOUDED ISAAC'S EXPRESSION. How she wanted to kiss that little furrow between his dark brows. Kiss every little bit of him, and hold him tight, and make him laugh. She had joked about bringing him back to life, and never imagined that his touch would bring her back to life—those vibrant, joyous parts of her that had been buried so long she'd forgotten they were there.

She eased off him and tumbled onto her back, and trailed a finger over his ribs.

"Your turn now," she said.

"My turn. Right."

With lightning speed, he was arranging himself over her, bumping her knees, mumbling a curse.

"Your legs," he muttered. "They're everywhere. Have you sprouted more of them?"

"Still just the usual number."

"They're in the way."

"Oh dear. Shall we remove them?"

"Not a chance. They're lovely legs." He hooked one of them over his shoulder and brushed his lips over her thigh. "Such a lovely leg." Then he blinked at it. "Look at that," he said, on a note of wonder, like an explorer discovering a hidden paradise. "Your leg does that."

"It does," she agreed. "Although not often and not recently enough for that to be comfortable. It seems I need practice too."

She shifted, with a little grunt, to wrap both her legs around his waist.

"How's that?"

He laughed. "This seems to be rather graceless and awkward. Or am I just not…"

"You're doing beautifully," she said honestly. "We are people, and people are messy, so why should we not be honest about that? I'm enjoying myself very much."

"I am too. You too are doing beautifully."

He slowly lowered his face to hers, but in the heartbeat before their mouths met, she thought she saw something in his eyes—or perhaps the something was inside her. Yearning ricocheted through her, sharp and bittersweet. She palmed the muscles in his back, as if she could capture his vigor and essence and hold it with her for all time.

"Do you think you can find your own way this time?" she whispered.

"I'm renowned for my powers of investigation," he rasped. "I'm sure I'll locate the appropriate place."

He took himself in hand and, craning his neck, guided himself into her.

Almost immediately, his face changed, as if he had witnessed a miracle.

"Look at that, we fit," he breathed.

"We do. We really do."

He understood what to do next, those instincts kicking

in. It felt wonderful, though Sylvia had lost his attention, as he focused on his own movement and pleasure. She didn't mind, because it was his first time, and she had already won an excellent climax from him, and there was such pleasure in this too, in his smooth, strong strokes, and his hot satiny skin, and his rippling muscles and scent, and the tickle of his hair. She gripped him more tightly with her legs, squeezed him when he entered her, congratulated herself that she could make him groan, make his eyes widen, make her own pleasure swell again. But it was not long before he tensed, shuddered, and released himself with a roar.

He stared at her, as if stricken, then collapsed onto the narrow mattress beside her. She slid her arms around him; he slid his around her.

"Sylvia," he mumbled as he pulled her closer, melding their damp skin and racing hearts.

"Yes?" she prompted, when he said nothing more.

"Yes," he groaned. "Yes and yes and yes."

CHAPTER 12

Sylvia wriggled her legs against the sheets and giggled softly to herself. The curtains were open and the fire was lit, the maid having already been in this morning—oh, how decadent her days had become!—and she sighed at the shimmering silver of the new winter's day.

That tryst with Isaac yesterday— Dear heaven, she had truly done that! She could hardly believe it of herself. Yet she felt renewed, youthful, hopeful. She couldn't remember feeling like this since…

Since the early days of her marriage to Michael, when their future looked bright, safe, and happy, and she'd believed in him so wholly she had never even thought to question it.

An unexpected jolt of fear had her throwing back the blankets and leaping out of bed. She had placed her future in Michael's hands— Well, a woman had no choice. A wife depended upon her husband to treat her future with care. Excitement and pleasure were all very well, but, in the end, they had not made her safe.

Mercifully, the maid chose that moment to arrive with fresh water, providing a happy distraction. As she dressed, Sylvia's eyes fell on the latest letter from Graham, pages of minute details on how he was sleeping poorly and feeling the chill and how Mrs. Yates the housekeeper had rearranged the furniture to suit him better. "*You may choose to make further changes, as suits us both,*" he had added graciously, "*but for now, our housekeeper displays a very pleasing sensitivity to my needs, and you will be glad to know I am in such good hands.*"

Guilt washed over her anew. She was behaving terribly, and the fact that Graham would never know—that no one would ever know—did little to salve her conscience. *I'll be a good wife to him,* she vowed to her reflection. *I'll give him every ounce of my attention and care and loyalty. I'll put his comfort above my own.*

But the bright-eyed woman in the mirror was almost a stranger; even her skin seemed to glow and her hair looked lustrous. And that stranger in the mirror said, "Yes, yes, but not yet."

Oh, but she was a terrible person, she thought as she dashed out of her bedroom. And foolish, foolish, foolish. Feeling free and young was as addictive as a fine wine or cake. How easy it was to forget her struggles, now she was warm again, and well clothed and well fed. *Don't get carried away,* she scolded herself. *Don't lose sight of the bigger picture.* This was nothing but a short respite, and however much she enjoyed Isaac, it was only an affair.

An affair, she decided, was like a game of Snapdragon. Heady, sweet treats were on offer, but one had to snatch them from the flames, which meant there was always the risk of getting burned. On the other hand, one might get a raisin with a button inside, and be granted a boon. And so help her, but Isaac DeWitt was definitely a boon.

MERCIFULLY, she didn't encounter him in the breakfast room, and happily joined the others at the table in a discussion of the weather.

As she pushed back her chair, Miss Babworth was suddenly at her side.

"Will you take a turn in the garden with me, Mrs. Ray?" she asked.

"I had meant to write some letters."

"Oh, please, do walk with me."

Miss Babworth seemed anxious, so Sylvia agreed. Once dressed warmly, they headed out into the garden, glistening and white under a fresh cover of snow.

The gardens at Sunne Park were famed in the middle of England and attracted visitors for much of the year. She knew from Mr. Joshua DeWitt's boasting that the garden was his wife's pride and joy, and as his wife was apparently *his* pride and joy, he spoke as if Sunne Park had the best garden in England, if not the world.

Cassandra and her husband were strolling in the garden too. He was speaking animatedly, waving his hands, while his two dogs wrestled each other, kicking up clouds of snow.

Sylvia would have greeted them, but her companion steered her away.

"I seek your advice, Mrs. Ray." Miss Babworth's eyes were fixed on the snowy path before them. "Do you remember on Christmas Eve, when you climbed a tree and Mr. Isaac rescued you?"

Images danced through Sylvia's mind: Isaac laughing at her, throwing her over his shoulder. Isaac naked on top of her, his body entangled with hers. She blinked the images away and took a cooling breath of air. It was a beautiful garden, and a fine day, and there was pleasant company to be had. But right now, she wanted only to be ensconced in that little cabin, on that narrow bed, far from reality and entirely engulfed in him.

"I suppose," she said, managing an indifferent tone.

"Lettie said you'd done it deliberately. Got stuck so Mr. Isaac would rescue you."

Sylvia stopped walking, stunned by the charge against her. Done it *deliberately*?

"She said it was very clever of you, for you had very good … seduction techniques," Miss Babworth blurted out, a blush staining her cheeks as she swallowed desperately.

The girl's discomfort had Sylvia shaking her head. Maybe being young was not to be envied after all.

"I assure you, there was nothing planned or deliberate that day. And I certainly don't—"

"I want to learn," Miss Babworth interrupted. "Seduction techniques."

"Miss Babworth, I don't think—"

"I scolded Lettie at the time. Said it was disrespectful and terribly rude to assume that every young widow is— you know. What some people say about young widows."

Sylvia made a noncommittal sound and tried to school her face to virtuous neutrality. Look at her, acting the innocent, when she had made all the cliches come true by seducing a younger man.

"But maybe Lettie was right," Miss Babworth went on. "Mr. Isaac seems to like you. He looks at you differently to how he looks at me. And he can't want you, not to marry, I mean. You're old and you're engaged. But you did something to him, and I would very much like to know how I can do that too. Please teach me."

Good heavens. It seemed her skills as a teacher were greatly in demand!

Sylvia made a show of casually brushing some snow off a plant and admiring the leaves. So much for discretion, if even this naive young woman had noticed.

At dinner the night before, she and Isaac had exchanged glances and secret smiles. Who knew what stories her face had been telling, given the way desire had curled through her. Desire for her paramour, her younger lover! She had sat in the respectable drawing room, making respectable conversation and hugging to herself the secret delight of being a brazen wanton for the first and only time in her life. She liked the way he looked at her, knowing, admiring, almost smug. It felt like a privilege, to induct this curious, adventurous, resourceful young man into carnal pleasures.

"I really don't know what you mean," Sylvia lied. "I know nothing of seduction techniques. I simply try to deal with people honestly. Spend time with Mr. Isaac and see how you like each other."

Miss Babworth made a discontented sound. "I'm twenty years old, and I fear I'll never marry. I thought I had good prospects. But 'tis all coming to naught."

"Are there no men of your acquaintance with an interest in you?"

She waved a hand dismissively. "One or two, I suppose."

"Are they terrible prospects?"

"They're fine," she said irritably. "And I might've chosen Mr. Moffat, the young squire, for he's easy to talk to and he has a fine farm, until I met Mr. Isaac. Oh, Mrs. Ray, there's no man on Earth so handsome or dashing as Mr. Isaac. His father's an earl, and he has sailed the world.

Mama says he's not quite respectable for he's illegitimate, but I care nothing for that. He's the one I want, not Mr. Moffat and his cows, and I'm growing quite mad with trying to get his attention. I thought he liked me, I thought he wanted to kiss me, but then…" She sighed. "It all came to naught."

Viewed one way, Sylvia had stolen Isaac from Prudence. Good heavens! She had become *that woman*.

She could have managed it differently, she supposed. Instead of kissing Isaac, she could have helped steer the young couple together. Instead, she had been piqued by him calling her *safe*; to be honest with herself, she'd felt a simmering attraction from the first time she laid eyes on him, which must have influenced her behavior.

But she knew Isaac wished to marry someone like Prudence Babworth. And in truth, she hadn't stolen him from anyone. She was merely training him to be a good husband to someone else.

It was not too late to guide Isaac and Prudence to each other, at least until each figured out what they wanted. In fact, it was probably better that she did. Her own infatuation with Isaac was almost overwhelming; as enjoyable as these feelings were, she must take care not to lose sight of reality.

"The most important thing is to be yourself and talk to him," she said.

"That sounds boring and too simple," Miss Babworth protested. "Don't I need wiles? And tricks?"

"You would hardly want to trick a man into marriage," Sylvia said, with another stab of guilt. Was she tricking Graham? Not at all. They both knew exactly what they were getting.

"But Mr. Isaac is not an ordinary man," Miss

Babworth argued. "What you're saying makes sense for *ordinary* men."

"Ordinary men such as Mr. Moffat, who is easy to talk to, owns a fine farm, and has an interest in you that you, until recently, returned?"

Miss Babworth missed the dryness of her tone. "Exactly," she said earnestly. "Ordinary conversation is all very well for them, but for Mr. Isaac—Eep!"

At her squeak, Sylvia followed her gaze. There he was, Isaac himself. His greatcoat flapped about his boots as he headed unwaveringly for them, and he seemed strong and serious under his hat, the light outlining the angles of his face. She caught a glimpse of the man he would become, in his thirties and forties and fifties, a man to be reckoned with, completely in command of himself. What a shame she would not know him then. He would never forget her, at least. She would certainly never forget him.

As he advanced, she felt rooted to the spot, and warm despite the cold. She concentrated on the iciness of the air entering her nostrils.

Too much, she thought.

She wanted him too much. Yearned for more. He belonged to Prudence Babworth, or some young lady like her; Sylvia was only borrowing him for a week or two.

A smile danced over Isaac's lips as he reached them. "Good morning, ladies. Miss Babworth," he added, as she murmured "Mr. Isaac" and lowered her chin to peer up at him through her lashes. The coquettish manner didn't suit her, or Isaac's tastes. The girl would do better if she didn't try so hard.

Then his eyes met hers.

"Mrs. Ray," he murmured.

And she was just as addled, by her longing to slide her

arms around his neck and lock her legs around his waist and lose herself in his terrible jokes and heart-melting smile.

"Mr. Isaac," she said, sounding suitably cool. "We were just wondering if we might encounter you today."

He blinked. "You were?"

"Miss Babworth wished to ask you about…" She glanced about for inspiration. "The construction of the folly," she improvised wildly.

"I did?" Miss Babworth's confusion matched the look in Isaac's eyes.

"You did," Sylvia said firmly. "And you had hoped that Mr. Isaac might guide you to it and offer some explanations."

Isaac's eyes narrowed. He claimed not to always understand women's conversation, but he understood this.

Miss Babworth caught on a heartbeat later. "Yes!" she gushed. "I really hoped you would walk with me to the folly."

"Do go ahead," Sylvia made herself say. "I can act as chaperone."

"Chaperone," he repeated flatly.

She met his gaze steadily. He was frowning. She had tried to think of him as young, much younger than her, and certainly his eagerness, vulnerability, and lack of guile suggested a certain boyishness. But under his gaze now, serious and focused, it was clear that Isaac DeWitt was no child, unversed in the world. Indeed, his experience of the world was much broader than her own, and he had dealt with a much broader range of people than she would ever meet. He understood enough about people to understand what she was doing.

Then he offered Miss Babworth a charming smile and one elbow. "I'd be delighted to discuss the folly with you."

Without hesitation, Prudence slipped her hand through that elbow and returned his smile. Off they went, down the path toward the folly, not looking back at Sylvia as she trailed after them, at an appropriate distance, just as an older widow and chaperone should.

CHAPTER 13

S he did not walk alone for long, though. At the sound of her name, she spun with a smile to greet Lady Charles, who emerged from a side path carrying a basket laden with laurel and sage.

"Good morning, my dear," Lady Charles said. "It seems everyone is out here today."

"The day is fine and the snow is sparkling," Sylvia observed, as they fell into step and meandered along the path. "We cannot help ourselves, I suspect, frail humans drawn to the scene the way a bee is drawn to a flower."

"You're walking alone? My apologies for neglecting you. I should have invited you to join me, but I was up so much earlier."

"Not at all. Miss Babworth was my companion, but alas, she was stolen away by a dashing young man." She gestured to where Miss Babworth and Isaac had reached the folly, apparently conversing with ease.

"What a shame," Lady Charles said lightly. "There is nothing like the company of young people to make one feel young."

"But this is how it ought to be," Sylvia said, as if to convince herself. "The lovely young unmarried creatures can enjoy each other's company, and the older sensible widows can keep an eye on them, in case their state of being lovely, young, and unmarried interferes with their good sense."

Pursing her lips, Lady Charles made an unnecessary adjustment to the herbs in her basket. "And you are content with that?"

"It is the way it ought to be," Sylvia repeated stolidly.

Her friend looped her spare arm through Sylvia's and continued their stroll, clearly unconcerned about chaperoning Isaac and Prudence.

"One of the oddest things about growing old is that, inside, I don't feel much different to how I felt when I was twenty," Lady Charles mused. "I know when young people look at me, they see a woman approaching fifty, a grandmother now, pottering around in her still room making strangely flavored wines, and who sometimes bores everyone with stories about balls and fashions in the previous century. 'Tis as though they can't possibly conceive that I was once young and beautiful and reckless, that I married twice, that I have gossiped at court and dined with royalty and seen—and perhaps even done—things that would make these young ones blush," she added with an arch look. "It sometimes feels that young people can't imagine that we women remain individuals as we age and do not suddenly transform into a shapeless mass of 'old tabbies.' Yet these are the same young people who imagine the world is ending if they get a spot on one cheek. They don't see us dashing about having affairs, and so they imagine we never did. Or might, indeed, be doing so now."

She paused, her words lingering in the air between them like the little clouds made by their breaths.

Sylvia expelled a shot of nervous anxiety in the form of a light laugh.

"Lady Charles, do tell," she teased. "Are you dashing about having an affair?"

"I'm not, alas. I have assessed our male guests and found them lacking." She paused. "But I'm not the only widow at Sunne Park."

Sylvia stopped short and turned to meet her friend's questioning gaze.

But of course. If naive Prudence Babworth had sensed something between her and Isaac, Lady Charles would have sensed and understood an awful lot more. Of course she would not be deceived by a couple of hapless fools fumbling their way through their first illicit affair.

Sylvia was not used to such goings on. It was said that affairs were de rigueur in the fancy houses of the aristocracy. What an odd thought, that she was behaving thus too: staying in the house of a duke's granddaughter and running around with that granddaughter's brother-in-law. She might be behaving as immorally as an aristocrat, but she was far too middle class to be blasé about it.

"Isaac is a handsome young man, isn't he?" Lady Charles added.

"He's very easy on the eyes."

"He seems to enjoy looking at you, too."

Embarrassment slithered over her. "I'm behaving badly," she blurted out. "Do forgive me. I'm here as your guest, and I am so grateful for the warm welcome from your whole family, and—"

"Hush, dear." Lady Charles squeezed her arm. "I didn't mean to scold. Only to warn you. It's Isaac, mainly, the way he looks at you. He has rather expressive eyes.

Perhaps you might advise him to be more discreet. I certainly cannot speak to him of it."

Sylvia closed her eyes and breathed deeply.

"My dear Mrs. Ray—Sylvia—do not fear my judgment. I'm difficult to shock and slow to criticize. No situation is straightforward and simple, for all that many people insist upon rigid standards of behavior without even trying to understand the context. Curiously, the people who are swiftest to judge are often the very same ones who are the first and loudest to proclaim their own compassion and empathy."

She walked on, holding Sylvia's arm as she continued.

"When we find ourselves in a difficult situation, we must deal with it as best we know how, as our needs and experiences and characters dictate, with the resources available to us. What would our critics do in the same situation? They are always so *certain* they would act with perfect virtue and remain ever above reproach."

Sylvia snorted. "Perhaps they wouldn't put themselves into that situation in the first place."

"Do any of us imagine we would?" Lady Charles sighed. "Desire and duty will ever compete, as will need and want. Perhaps one man can give you what you need to survive, but you must turn to another for what you need to thrive, and such are the delicate, difficult situations our lives are made of, the dilemmas we face as we navigate through our days. Do not fear me for a moral critic; I have no patience with those who insist upon rigid values and willfully fail to consider the context in which people act."

"Thank you," Sylvia said shakily. "I'm sure what I'm doing is wrong and yet…"

"And yet you have had some difficult years and you need something sweet for yourself, to revive your soul, as it were."

Tears pricked Sylvia's eyes at her friend's kindness. She fished out a kerchief and swiped them away.

"Lady Charles, I don't wish to lose your good opinion. Your friendship means so much to me."

"I cherish our friendship too. I've lost much in recent years and gained many regrets. Distilling wines and cordials has given me a fresh interest. Perhaps you don't realize how much your generosity with your time and skills has meant to me. But I must be sure you understand that Isaac is not what he appears."

Sylvia twisted the kerchief around her fingers. Sounds of laughter bounced over the snow: Miss Lettie, Emily, and Jane had joined Miss Babworth and Isaac in the folly, where they swung off the columns.

"I know," she said.

"He had to grow up very fast, and he is both man and boy. A man who has sailed the world and survived situations most of us couldn't even imagine, yet a boy who longs for a settled home and does not know how to make that happen."

"He is not such a boy," Sylvia said.

"Isaac wants a wife. He wants an anchor, of sorts." She squeezed Sylvia's arm meaningfully. "He is not a man who takes relationships lightly, because he has had so few of them."

"I wouldn't call myself sophisticated either," Sylvia confessed. "But Isaac and I have an understanding."

Back at the folly, Miss Babworth had abandoned Isaac to join the other ladies. He was striding back toward Sylvia.

"We've discussed our situation at length," she went on, dragging her eyes off Isaac's stern, unsmiling face. "We've agreed on the parameters."

"Very well. If you're sure." Lady Charles shot her a

knowing look. "But do warn him to hide that expression in his eyes when he looks at you."

Then Lady Charles showed her how it was done, turning to smile at Isaac as if he had not been the subject of their conversation. He didn't look at Sylvia as he doffed his hat to Lady Charles, who rose up on her toes and pressed a light kiss to his cheek.

"What was that for?" he asked. "Not complaining, but wondering what it is I've done, that I may do it again and earn a kiss like that every day."

"Oh, you charmer," she said, then with a bland smile at no one in particular, she excused herself and left them alone.

CHAPTER 14

As soon as Lady Charles was out of earshot, Isaac turned to scowl at Sylvia.

"I wish to talk to you." His tone came out flat and hard. Well, he *felt* flat and hard. "Now."

He hauled her toward the shrubbery. His conversation with Miss Babworth had been quite amiable, and quite dull, and he'd been quite relieved when she was swept off by the other young ladies. He'd been even more relieved not to keep smiling and being agreeable when he wasn't in the mood, not after what Sylvia had done.

"Isaac, be careful," she hissed as he pulled her along the icy path between the high hedges.

He slowed his pace, for he didn't wish her to fall on the ice, but he had misunderstood again, for with the next breath, she added, "We must be more discreet. People are noticing."

He released her and spun around. The hedges loomed over them, sheltering them from the world.

"You fobbed me off on Prudence Babworth. You made

yourself *chaperone*," he said, indignant on her behalf, as if someone had slighted her. As far as he could tell, *she* had.

"'Tis the way of the world," she said, chin raised defiantly. "You are courting, and the older widow must—"

"No." His denial was swift. She blinked at him, her lovely mouth still open from her unspoken words. "It is not the way of *my* world. In my world, you are not the sort of older widow who hovers around the edges. In my world, you are the sort who lures an innocent young man into a warm cabin and has her wicked way with him. That *was* you, wasn't it, Sylvia?" he added on a lower murmur. "I've not mistaken you for some other welcoming woman, have I? That was your naked body under mine in the cabin yesterday, wasn't it?"

Something flared in her eyes. Faint pink stained her cheeks. Had he angered her? Or shamed her? But—Bloody hell! Making herself *chaperone*! Relegating herself to the edges like some faded, withering wallflower! She of the gentle humor and practical nature and surprisingly strong and silky thighs.

"It's what you wanted," she spluttered. "You wanted to court her, and she wants you to court her, so I was providing an opportunity for you. To teach you to court—"

"No. I can't court her while I'm thinking of you. And I can't stop thinking of you."

"Then perhaps it's better we end this now."

Her soft words slammed into him like the recoil of a shotgun. "You want to end it?"

"Not at all," she said quickly. "But you—you mustn't forget this is only an affair."

"I know what this is. But one afternoon doesn't make an affair. I'm not clear on the exact definition, but surely one must have at least three trysts for it to qualify as an affair."

"Three?" she repeated, tilting her head.

On reflection, three wasn't nearly enough. "At least twenty," he amended.

Twenty would be enough, wouldn't it? Yes, surely.

Finally, she smiled, eyes alight with that appealing gentle humor. The fur of her coat brushed her chin, and he imagined sliding his fingers into the warm spot there.

"You have no need for twenty trysts to learn to bed a woman," she said. "You're confident by nature, and observant and curious, and you'll acquit yourself admirably. I said I'd teach you, and I've taught you enough. You don't need me anymore."

"But I still want you." He stepped closer, backing her against a hedge, taking a new, fierce pleasure in the way she swallowed nervously. "I can't stop thinking about it, what we did together. How wonderful it was. How wonderful *you* were." He ran one hand over her shoulder, reveling in her solidity. "I thought I'd go mad last night, sitting across from you at dinner, playing parlor games in the drawing room. Wanting to touch you and kiss you. I could hardly sleep for desperately craving you. *Craving* you, yet not barging into your room because you've made a stupid rule forbidding it."

Surrendering to temptation, he removed a glove and feathered his fingertips over her jaw.

"We've established that I'm lacking experience in intimate relationships with women, so perhaps I have this wrong," he said slowly, "but I would've thought that if I were truly inclined toward Prudence Babworth, you wouldn't prove such a powerful distraction. If you don't truly wish to end it for yourself, then it's not right to push me on her. It's not fair to her, or to me, or to you. When I came to meet you this morning, I hardly even noticed who you were with. All I could see was you."

She shifted awkwardly. "Yet, if we're sensible, we can see I have a powerful advantage over Prudence. You've seen me naked and you have a very good chance of doing that again."

"I have seen you naked," he agreed, his voice coming out low and rough at her implicit promise: He would get to see her naked again! He eased closer. "By some astonishing miracle, I've been inside you."

At his words, her expression changed as if he'd fired a cannonball at her. Her eyes widened and darkened, her cheeks stained, her lips parted. Had he insulted her? An apology formed on his lips. But no. Given the heat under his own skin and the dryness of his own parted lips—He'd wager it was not anger he had aroused.

Smug satisfaction bloomed in his chest.

"Well, well, well," he murmured. "I'm learning more all the time. What an excellent teacher you are. It seems my words alone can affect my lover. Is that right?"

"It appears to be the case, yes." She gulped. "It seems I'm learning new things too."

"Then let me see if I've grasped the lesson." He ran a thumb over her lips. "I think you liked that reminder, that I have been inside you."

"Mm."

"Interesting. That's much the same sound you made when I was in—"

"Isaac," she gasped. "Enough."

He chuckled. "Is it, though? I, for one, have definitely not had enough of you."

He gripped her waist. A tremble ran through her body.

"Are you cold?"

"I'm merely— Oh dear, there is nothing mere about it."

"Good." He cupped a breast, somehow finding the

softness under the thick layers of wool. "Now, what else might I say to make you quiver with desire for me?"

"You are terrible," she breathed.

"I am," he agreed happily. "But surely with lots of practice, I'll get better. Let me tell you this: At dinner last night, I kept picturing you naked. I was remembering how lovely your breasts looked in the candlelight, how perfect they felt in my hands, how much I wanted to taste them. Every time you took a sip of wine, I imagined your lips on my naked skin."

She rested her forehead on his shoulder, and her hands darted inside his greatcoat to spread over his chest. He'd never imagined speaking to a woman like this, nor that an affair would involve such delightful moments of intimacy and play. But then it also involved those unpleasant moments when she fobbed him off on another woman under misguided reasoning. Never had he dreamed that a single tryst could change so much. That an affair could be more than furtive grappling in the dark.

"How am I doing?" he murmured against her ear.

"So terrible," she whispered.

"More practice is required, then. What shall I say next?"

"I'm not sure I can cope with anymore."

"That bad?"

When she looked up at him, a new glint sparked in her eyes. Her teeth snagged her lower lip, just long enough for fresh desire to cannonball through him, before she rose up on her toes, pressing against his chest to balance herself.

Then she whispered in his ear. "It's too cold for me to take you inside me here, so it's not fair to make me want you so much."

Every part of him stiffened, and he groaned, a deep,

guttural sound of longing. He spun away from her, his groan breaking into a frustrated laugh.

"Once more the teacher outdoes the student." He glanced at her. "How about this: If I sit on the bench, then—"

The sounds of girlish chatter intruded through the shrubbery. Isaac froze, listening, then cursed.

"I think they're coming this way." He swore again. "And here I am in agony, an unfit state for conversation with anyone other than you."

Sylvia patted his shoulder. "That's what you get for starting this. Lesson learned?"

He flashed a grin. "No regrets. It was worth it to watch your face change when I said—"

A shriek of laughter ricocheted around them.

"Shall I toss you over my shoulder and run away?" he asked.

She giggled. "We can try."

Holding hands, they began to run, but she soon slipped and they had to stop, trying to hold each other upright, smothering their laughter, which only made them want to laugh more.

"We're not going to make it," she whispered. "Find me later. But Isaac, you must take care. How you look at me. Your eyes say too much. People are noticing. They guess."

"I can't stop looking at you. Not when I want more. Tonight," he murmured. "Can we forget your stupid rule?"

The girls were close enough now that their words could be made out.

"Yes," she said, and Isaac slipped away, through a gap in the shrubbery, his hands feeling bereft of her.

Behind him came the young ladies' shrieks of delight as they greeted Sylvia with such buoyant enthusiasm one might think she was the first human they had seen in months.

Isaac polished the miniature table and slid it back into the dollhouse's dining room. He admired the setting, until the tick of the clock pulled him back to the real world.

The afternoon was dragging. A turn in the weather kept him inside, where at least the dollhouse was proving diverting.

Diverting from the questions swirling in his head like the snow outside. When Sylvia suggested ending their affair, had she actually meant it, but was being polite? Or did she not want to end the affair, but was giving him the option to end it if he wanted to? What if she had wanted to end the affair, but he had distracted her with his talk? What had she meant? What the hell had she meant?

"The curtains are faded," he said to Joshua, who was experimenting with a tiny pulley system for the dollhouse.

Isaac laid the little curtains over one palm, poking at their faded stripes. "Would Cassandra have some scraps of fabric? I could sew new curtains."

Joshua didn't look up. "You know how to sew curtains?"

"All sailors know how to sew."

"Yes, but do you know how to sew adorable little curtains for a dollhouse that will please my daughter in a few years?"

"I'll figure it out," Isaac said. "I figure out all sorts of things. Most recently I figured out——"

He stopped short.

Joshua shot him an impatient look. "What? What?"

How to touch a woman to give her pleasure. How to

talk to a woman to make her want more. How to undo the fastenings on a woman's dress. And—here was a triumph—how to *do her dress back up again.*

"Nothing," he muttered. He flapped the little curtains. "Joshua?"

"What?"

"How can you know what women are thinking?"

"Ask them."

"But if you ask them, how can you be sure they'll answer straight?"

"They won't. Most people's thinking isn't straight, so how are they supposed to express what they're thinking if they don't even know it themselves?" Joshua shoved his invention aside. "Do you always know what you're thinking?"

Point made. And even when Isaac thought he knew what he was thinking, his thinking changed without him realizing it.

For example, a few days ago he'd been thinking that Prudence Babworth might make him a good wife. It had seemed so urgent and important, this need to find a wife.

Now, that urgency was gone. Now what seemed urgent was getting Sylvia alone again. One tryst! A single tryst! How the hell could that ever be enough? How did other men sleep with a woman only once? Sylvia's body was fascinating. And the sensations! Surely they'd only begun to scratch the surface of the possibilities. Maybe other men didn't enjoy themselves as much as Isaac had with Sylvia, or perhaps he was merely moonstruck because she was his first. Perhaps other men were just as delighted their first time, and then they tired of it. He hoped he never tired of it.

But what if Sylvia was already tired of him? What if that was why she had suggested ending it?

Ask her. Damn. That was the only way.

Frustration smothered him again. He didn't know this sort of frustration, or this ravenous restlessness that made him want to hunt her down and kiss her and shake her all at once. This was part of it too, he suspected. Affairs came with new feelings and awkward conversations. Perhaps *that* was why some men preferred brothels and mistresses and quick clandestine couplings—not because they grew bored, but to avoid having to *talk*.

It was all very well to say that one should express one's thoughts and feelings, but such advice assumed, first, that one knew one's own thoughts and feelings, and, second, that expressing those thoughts and feelings would not just make everything worse.

"Do you always know what you're thinking?" he asked Joshua, as Cassandra came in, holding Rose against her shoulder.

"Always," Joshua said promptly. "Though I'm usually thinking about twenty different things. If I'm not sure what I'm thinking, Cassandra will tell me. Saves me a lot of trouble, not wasting time figuring out my own thoughts, when my wife can do it for me. Isn't that right, my love?" he said to Cassandra. "What am I thinking now?"

Their eyes met. Isaac noticed how his sister-in-law's expression changed, just a little, as if she had indeed read her husband's thoughts. That communion between two people: How did one get *that*?

"Mrs. DeWitt!" Joshua said. "I am shocked you might think I'm thinking such a thing."

Pink rose in Cassandra's cheeks. Isaac tossed the curtains aside, muttered a hasty, "I'll be off, then," and escaped out the door.

CHAPTER 15

Sylvia gripped her book and stared at the bed. Reading in bed had long been one of her little pleasures, losing herself in some silly young woman's Gothic adventures, when she was fortunate enough to pick up a book for a spare penny. During the hard years, she'd not been able to spare the candles to read at night, so she'd huddled in the dark and put herself to sleep by recalling stories she'd read in the past.

Now, when luxuries abounded—access to a full library, candles, a warm bed—her mind was instead on a door down the hall.

She wanted to see him.

Isaac had heeded her warning and been suitably remote all evening. She'd known why, but it had stung all the same. A secret affair was exciting, true, but how much better to be open in one's affections, like Mr. and Mrs. DeWitt.

Did she dare go see him?

A light tap at her door: She jumped. Hastily, she

dropped the book, smoothed down her nightgown, and whispered a hoarse "Come in?"

Isaac slipped through the door as silent as the night, then closed it and locked it with a tiny click. He wore only his shirt and breeches, as if he were interrupted while undressing for bed; he must have been freezing until he reached her warm room.

A half-smile played over his lips as he took in the sight of her modest winter nightgown. His eyes fell on her long, thick plait, hanging over one shoulder.

"You have *hair*," he said on a note of wonder.

"I do have hair," she agreed solemnly.

And just like that, the odd tension was broken. He came close enough to wrap the end of her plait around his hand.

"I want to see it loose," he said.

"I want to see yours loose."

Neither moved. He studied her plait a moment longer before he spoke.

"You mentioned at some point," he started, "that everything will go well with my future wife so long as I talk to her and so forth."

Something about his words made her uneasy. She hugged herself.

"Marry someone you can talk to, someone who listens," she said. "She'll talk to you, too, if she feels safe and comfortable with you."

"Could you talk to your husband?"

She hesitated, then said, "He dismissed my cares as if they were nothing. If I persisted, he grew irritated, and so I learned to stay silent."

"I want you to feel comfortable with me."

"I do."

His eyes held hers. "Then you'll tell me honestly: When

you suggested earlier that we end this, did you actually mean that you want to end it?"

"No." Her voice came out too loud. "No," she repeated, more softly. "I wished only to check that we're still in agreement about what we're doing and why."

"You have doubts?"

"Only that... It might no longer be in your best interests. If your dearest wish is to marry, then an affair with me will obstruct that goal. I wouldn't want you to lose sight of your long-term needs for the sake of some short-term pleasure. Or to confuse our intimacy with more lasting feelings."

It seemed ridiculous to even think it. Sylvia was usually sensible, and the fact was, she was still safe for Isaac. She offered him a no-risk, no-judgment way to explore a woman's body, without fearing that she might humiliate him or manipulate him or break his heart. If she hadn't happened upon that debacle with Miss Babworth on Christmas Eve, if she hadn't kissed him in the woods, he would never have even noticed her as a woman, let alone be sneaking into her room at night or trying to seduce her in the shrubbery. She didn't mind, she reminded herself. It had been her idea, because she wanted— How had Lady Charles phrased it? She wanted something sweet for herself.

But Lady Charles had issued a warning against hurting Isaac, and Sylvia felt honor bound to at least check.

He snapped his fingers. "Lady Charles," he said. "You were conversing with her this morning and then you sought to end our affair."

"She's guessed. It was she who told me to warn you about your expressive eyes. She worries you might not understand about affairs and that I'm taking terrible advantage of your innocence."

"But I like you taking advantage of my innocence, and the more terrible the better. Lady Charles is rather protective of me. She lost a son and just as she was emerging from her grief, I was there. She likes to mother me, and I don't object. Even for a man of my age, it's nice to have a mother, for I've not seen my own mother since I was ten." His voice lowered. "But Lady Charles isn't here with us, and I don't want you to mother me. Are your feelings for me maternal?"

"Good heavens, no, not in the slightest."

"I'm very glad to hear it. Because you're insulting me by suggesting I'm not a man of my word."

Her chin jerked up. "I am?"

"We had an agreement." He inched closer, her hair still wrapped around his hand. He was more confident now she had spoken plainly. "As I recall, our arrangement had two parts. You would instruct me in— What shall we call it?— carnal pleasures. And I was to give you exciting memories, to make you feel young and carefree. Are you truly satisfied with only one tryst?"

"No," she whispered.

"Or are you bored with me already? Perhaps it isn't so exciting for a woman to be with a man who doesn't know what he's doing."

"I find it exciting to be with a man who's keen to listen to everything I say."

"I don't want to stop, Sylvia. Not yet."

"I don't want to stop either," she said, so save her for her wickedness. "But we must be clear. No one must get hurt or confused."

He seemed completely unconcerned. "Perfect. We have all the Christmas season. We'll go our separate ways but not yet. I don't want to marry the first woman who shows an interest in me, so let's do this first, and once you've gone off to get married, I can turn my attention to finding a bride."

"That's what we agreed," she said, forcing a smile, hoping he didn't detect the sudden sadness shadowing her heart.

Lady Charles's warning had been misdirected. It was not Isaac who needed a warning, but Sylvia. It was too easy to daydream, especially in the evenings, in that lovely warm drawing room amid welcoming company, when she had a full belly and the glow from a glass of wine— Yes, it was all too easy to let herself daydream that this, or something like it, might be real, and not a sweet, impossible interlude between the two harsher, drearier realities of her life.

He was playing with her hair again.

"You're very enthusiastic about my hair tonight," she observed.

"This amuses you?"

"Yesterday, you were very enthusiastic about my breasts."

"I'm still very enthusiastic about your breasts. I've learned I have a boundless capacity for enthusiasm when it comes to your body. Indeed, I'm learning all sorts of things I didn't even know were there to be learned. For example, I've learned I'm not a rake. There are men who wish to visit new lands merely to conquer them, but then there are men like me, who seek only to discover and explore." He slid the ribbon from the end of her plait and set about loosening her hair. "And there is so much more of you to explore. Are you a conqueror, and now you have me begging at your feet you have no need of me? Or are you an explorer like me?"

"Definitely an explorer."

"Every time I look at you, I find something new to be

fascinated by. I am an explorer and I have some exploring to do." He arranged her loose hair around her shoulders, then stepped back to draw off his shirt, his muscles shifting enticingly as he moved. "You are warm enough? Because I don't want you under the covers. I want to see you. All of you."

"You saw me yesterday," she said, as he tugged up her nightgown. "Nothing has changed."

"It might have. You might have grown a tail or an extra leg. I'll never know if you don't give me another look."

She let him pull the nightgown over her head, let him carry her to the bed.

"Yesterday was more of a reconnaissance mission," he said, in between pressing kisses to her mouth, her neck, her shoulders. "Now I need to make a full exploration, using my fingers, eyes, and mouth."

She laughed, burying her hands in his hair, taking the opportunity to release it. All the while, his hot, promising mouth roamed lower and lower over her body.

"Where are you going?" she asked. "What are you doing?"

"I want to see your whatchamacallit. Your button."

"My button?"

His questing hand found the juncture of her thighs. "What do you call it?"

Embarrassment and desire burned inside as twin flames. "I don't call it anything."

"You have a magic button, and—"

"Oh, dear heaven, no. Do not call it a button."

"Why not?" He grinned at her. "Buttons are used to open things. I'll press your magic button to open your magic cave, and then I can put my magic sword—"

"That's terrible," she half laughed, half groaned. "Please stop talking now."

"I'm not entirely innocent," he said. "I've seen sketches. And now I understand what was happening in those sketches. If I can give you pleasure by touching you with my fingers, then surely I can give you pleasure with my mouth?"

She began to scramble away, but he caught her legs. "Why would you do that?" she asked.

"If you don't want me to talk, I'll have to find some better use for my mouth." Once more, he melted her with that rakish grin. "We are fellow explorers, are we not? Let's see what we discover together."

CHAPTER 16

In all his years at sea, Isaac had rarely seen sailors watch the weather as closely as the ladies of Sunne Park watched it on the eve of the new year.

According to the almanac, there would be a full moon on the last night of the year, which, the ladies eagerly explained, made it ideal for a ball because the moonlight enabled nighttime travel. The annual tradition of tolling the bells to "ring in the new year" would not do. Rather, all of Longhope Abbey must "dance in the new year." To this end, a ball would be held at the neighboring estate of Vindale Court, hosted by Mr. and Lady Belinda Larke, and their daughter Arabella, now Lady Hardbury, and her husband the marquess.

So long as the skies remained clear.

But, as Joshua said, not even the weather dared quarrel with Arabella, Lady Hardbury. The clouds stayed away, and the bright moon was beaming down on the snow-covered gardens of Vindale Court as high-spirited parties tumbled out of carriages, ready to dance.

Isaac offered Sylvia his arm. No one seemed to think it

odd for him to escort her inside. Joshua escorted Cassandra, Lord Tidcombe accompanied Lady Charles, the engineers wandered in, looking puzzled as to why they were there, while the quartet of young ladies bounced along, their frothy white gowns gleaming in the moonlight.

Sylvia's ballgown was a blue-green color; it suited her very well. Pleasure had suffused Isaac's whole body when she traipsed down the stairs dressed for the ball, her hair twisted into ringlets, her eyes bright. It had been all he could do not to sweep her into his arms, right there in front of everyone.

The gown had belonged to Cassandra, a gift that Sylvia had warmly accepted as an offer of friendship; she didn't behave for one second as though Cassandra was giving her charity, or that the gift was a burden on either one. The pair of them had partnered on adjusting and trimming the gown with as much companionable excitement as if they were making choices at London's finest modiste. A new, odd warmth had burst through him at the sight of their heads bent together over ribbons and silk. Cassandra was one of Isaac's favorite people, and she loved making new friends. How wonderful of Sylvia to welcome her friendship.

Isaac had learned all about the ballgown while they were strolling one day by the lake, watching the teals paddle and dabble in the cold water. Sylvia had pointed at the teals and said, "Look, the bodice and trimmings on my ballgown are the same blue-green color as those ducks' faces!"

"And your hair is a similar color to their heads."

"A lesson in courting, Isaac," she had laughed. "'Tis not considered romantic to compare a lady to a duck. Swans and nightingales, yes. Ducks, no."

"Nonsense. Ducks are clever, hardy, and pretty, and you

will be the cleverest, hardiest, and prettiest little ducky at the ball."

She had then launched into a captivatingly enthusiastic monologue about her ballgown. He'd not understood one word in five, something about a "round dress" and "satin points" and a "single fall of blond," which, upon further questioning, turned out to be a sort of lace and not a yellow-haired woman with a balance problem.

Ducks and ballgowns, moonlight and lace: Isaac took pleasure in everything now, thanks to Sylvia. It strengthened his resolve to ensure that she, too, received everything she wanted.

If only he could claim credit for arranging the fine weather, just so he could claim credit for her awed expression when she stared up at the imposing towers of Vindale Court and its blazing lights.

"Good heavens," she whispered. "Is this the English residence of the Empress of Russia? Surely it's home to the empress of *somewhere*."

"It's the childhood home of the lady who's now Marchioness of Hardbury. She's grander than every empress in the world put together."

Sylvia cast him a stricken look. The pearls woven through her hair gleamed in the moonlight.

"My knees are trembling at the thought of meeting such a grand personage," she said. "How shall I dance before her with trembling knees? And I do so dearly want to dance."

"Lady Hardbury amuses herself by cultivating a fearsome manner, but I promise you, she's not unkind. At least, not to those whom she doesn't think deserves it. And she would never be rude to her guests, nor to someone of lower status. Come along, then."

They entered the house together, Isaac feeling absurdly proud of himself to have her clutching his arm, to be the one guiding her as her eyes volleyed hungrily over the other guests and she paid no attention to where she put her feet.

"Are there enough gentlemen, do you think?" she mused. "Or will this widow be a wallflower?"

"Not a chance. I'll make it my mission to ensure you dance every set."

She lowered her voice. "You can't dance more than one with me."

"And I shan't. At least, not at the ball." He leaned close and murmured, "Perhaps later I'll coax you into a different sort of dance."

She fought a smile, and he felt absurdly proud of himself for that too.

"What I meant," he said, once they had deposited their outerwear and joined the receiving line, "is that I shall ensure you have partners."

"But young ladies abound, and we mustn't forget I'm a widow on the wrong side of thirty, which means I'm destined to sit by a wall and glower judgmentally at the pretty young creatures for daring to enjoy themselves too much."

"I'll not permit you to put on a dowdy lace cap and retire to the edges. You may be a duck full grown, but you're as lively and lovely as any of these ducklings. You wish to feel young and have memories," he reminded her. "What better memory than dancing every set at a moonlit midwinter ball in one of the grandest estates in the middle of England?"

"That sounds marvelous," she sighed.

"This is your night, so tell me whom you want as your partner and I shall make it so."

"Ooh, what about that one?" she said, with a tiny jerk of her chin. "I want *him*."

Isaac followed her gaze to an impeccably dressed gentleman who was tall, brawny, and blond. An empty space circled him like a spotlight, as if no one dared to get too close.

"Congratulations," he said dryly. "You've chosen Lord Hardbury himself."

She bit her lip mischievously. "Is he too difficult a target? I chose him because he looks the grandest, but I can't expect you to ask favors from someone so grand."

"I'll procure him for you."

"How will you do that?"

Isaac hadn't the faintest idea. He claimed a slight acquaintance with Hardbury and liked him; the marquess had a down-to-earth manner despite his high status and intimidating appearance. But whereas Joshua would happily barrel up to anyone and make his demands, Isaac was less certain of his own standing. Certainly, it would be the height of impudence for him to ask a marquess to dance with a widow of no status.

But if it pleased Sylvia, he would try.

"Or maybe not," she whispered. "Is that tall, dark-haired lady his wife? The marchioness and our hostess? She looks so elegant and haughty that I'm terrified already. I daren't so much as glance twice at her husband for fear she'll smite me with a look."

Arabella, Lady Hardbury, was indeed looking intimidating. The young ladies filed solemnly past her as if they were tiptoeing past a sleeping wolf. Isaac hovered protectively at Sylvia's elbow as she was introduced.

But neither need fear the marchioness, who favored Sylvia with a gracious smile. "Mrs. Ray, Lady Charles has spoken very highly of your skills in the still room. She tells me you make a very welcome addition to Sunne Park this Christmas season."

Sylvia beamed with pleasure. Isaac felt a burst of warm gratitude to Lady Hardbury.

"Do you spend much time in your still room, my lady?" Sylvia asked politely, her voice a little shaky with nerves.

"Good grief, no. I'd probably poison someone." She pursed her lips. "Although now I think of it, could you recommend a simple recipe for a subtle and effective poison?"

Sylvia blinked, frozen, unsure.

Lord Hardbury rescued her with a chuckle. "Arabella," he said to his wife with mock sternness, "you are not going to run about poisoning anyone."

"Don't be absurd. I never run. If I were to poison someone, I'd do it at a more dignified pace. Besides, I'd only poison people who deserved it. And I'd most likely refrain from poisoning you, Hardbury," she assured her husband. "I've decided I'm still rather fond of you."

"How very comforting," he said dryly, his eyes crinkling with affectionate mirth.

Cassandra rejoined the conversation with a protective hand on Sylvia's arm. "Arabella, what dreadful thing have you said to poor Mrs. Ray? She looks quite stunned."

Lady Hardbury sniffed haughtily. "I've said nothing untoward. I merely invited her to give me a few lessons in making poisons."

Cassandra shook her head. "I wonder you would need lessons. I thought you already knew everything."

"Don't be absurd. It's impossible to know everything. I merely know more than everyone else."

Laughing, Cassandra led Sylvia away, saying something about "you must meet Freddie," and Lady Hardbury turned to greet the next guests.

Isaac quickly snared the marquess's attention. "Lord Hardbury, if I might impose on you a moment."

Hardbury raised a single eyebrow in response.

"Are you dancing tonight?" Isaac hurriedly asked.

"Is there such a shortage of ladies, DeWitt, that you must resort to inviting me to take a twirl with you?"

"I've undertaken to perform a service for Mrs. Ray: to ensure she has partners all night."

"Am I supposed to know who Mrs. Ray is?" He followed Isaac's gaze, to where Sylvia stood in a circle with Cassandra and some other ladies. "Ah, yes, Mrs. DeWitt's guest. The widow from Birmingham with the remarkable distillation skills who will teach my wife how to poison me." His gaze returned to Isaac. "You're asking me to dance with your widow?"

"Not *my* widow," he said hastily. "Did I say mine? No, not mine. Just *a* widow. Someone else's widow. She'd only be my widow if I'd married her and then died, neither of which I've done. So."

"You have no personal interest in this widow?"

"Absolutely, definitely not, sir," Isaac said. "I aim merely to render a service. If you wish, I could render you a service in exchange."

At that, Hardbury's brows drew together, his interest piqued.

"I hear good reports of your investigative skills," he said. "My office is investigating some irregular activity related to shipping in Liverpool. You're familiar with that area, aren't you? Perhaps you might look into something for me, in exchange for my dancing with this widow."

"Quite a large favor," Isaac said noncommittally.

"Quite a large number of ladies I could dance with," Hardbury countered.

"A waltz-sized favor, I'd say."

Hardbury released a low whistle. Uh oh. Had Isaac made too great an imposition on this powerful man? But a moment later, the powerful man was clapping him on the shoulder.

"Well played, DeWitt. If you show as much commitment and courage in carrying out your business obligations as you do in filling this lady's dance card, then I'll benefit greatly from our arrangement. I'll waltz with this widow tonight—the widow who is, as we have established, very definitely not yours and of no personal interest to you whatsoever—and you'll call on me two days hence."

After surviving his impudence with the most powerful man in the room, Isaac was much bolder in approaching other gentlemen, most of whom took his request to dance with Mrs. Ray as excellent sport. By the end of the evening, he owed a lot of favors, but it was more than worth it, to present to Sylvia a nearly full dance card.

Isaac's name appeared on it only once. As the first notes of music floated through the air for the opening dance, he bowed and led her onto the floor.

The opening dance was a slow one, a warm-up for the evening that allowed older couples to join. As the hosts, Lord and Lady Hardbury took their positions facing each other at the top of the line, their gazes locked in a compelling mix of amusement, affection, and challenge. Two rows lined up alongside them, men and women facing each other. Isaac found himself grinning at Sylvia as the dance began.

And herein another lesson: the true appeal of dancing. Each time his fingers touched Sylvia's, even through two layers of evening gloves, desire and possibility shimmered through him. Their eyes met, parted. Her skirts brushed his calves as she swirled past him. Then he would be facing another partner, touching someone else's hand, forcing himself to nod and smile and not turn to look at Sylvia. He always knew where she was, as if he had an internal compass pointing him toward her.

Ha! If he wanted to be crude, he could easily name the compass needle that was pointing right at her! Perhaps he would tell her that later, he thought, grinning at a surprised woman. Sylvia would groan at his terrible joke and tell him to stop talking, and he would happily turn his mouth to something more important, such as covering her lovely body in his kisses.

CHAPTER 17

When the dance ended, Isaac relinquished Sylvia to her next partner, and mingled through the ballroom.

He would probably not talk to her again this evening, but just knowing she was present was enjoyment enough, catching a glimpse of her animated face as she hopped and twirled and chatted, the blue-green bodice of her gown bringing out the sparkle in her eyes, the light from the chandelier burnishing her hair.

But every so often their eyes would meet, for no longer than a heartbeat, then she would carry on dancing and he would carry on conversing, all as if nothing had happened, but they both knew. Their shared experiences connected them. It made him feel as if there was more to him than just himself. Like when the crew of a ship worked together, each sailor with his own task, but always aware of everyone else. That was something he missed about life at sea, that feeling of being part of a crew, part of something bigger than himself. Never had he expected to find that feeling with a woman.

What a revelation.

These past days with Sylvia had been among the most delightful of his life. It was exquisite to brush his hand against hers when they passed in a corridor, to stand too close when they played parlor games, to corner her for a quick kiss in the shrubbery before running away like a mischievous boy. And after those secret touches and stolen kisses, when they were finally alone, they were all the more keen.

No matter how many times he touched Sylvia, he didn't grow tired of that touch. Even lying by her side, sated, was a delight. This boded well for his future, he decided. He was not a rake, and he'd be faithful when he finally chose a wife.

But he hadn't completely discharged his promise to her, and so he asked Joshua to dance the final unclaimed set with Sylvia, one of the more vigorous reels.

"Have you launched a new business procuring partners for ladies?" Joshua asked. "Or is this an exclusive service for Mrs. Ray?"

Isaac kept his expression bland. "I've set myself a challenge of ensuring she dances every set. She says it can't be done, and I'm determined to prove her wrong."

"And you've set her the challenge of dancing with me," Joshua said. "Will she survive that?"

"If Mrs. Ray is anything, she's a survivor."

But he complied cheerfully. Isaac stood with Cassandra to watch as Joshua, being Joshua, added extra spins and jumps to the figures, and soon had the dance floor in chaos and Sylvia almost helpless with laughter as she tried to keep up.

"I'm enjoying Mrs. Ray's company very much," Cassandra said. "She's proven a great friend to Mama, giving her exactly what she needs right now, and she's taught me things I never knew about the properties of some of my flowers."

"Yes, she's a great teacher," he murmured, hugging their secret to himself, as the young ladies joined them. Emily rested her head on Cassandra's shoulder, and the Babworth sisters sipped their drinks.

Bloody hell, but they were all so young, though technically of marriageable age. He couldn't imagine marrying anyone so young now. It was not the years themselves, he supposed, but experience. Experience shaped character and revealed much about how a person bore hardships and celebrated good times.

"You've only danced two sets, Mr. Isaac," Miss Lettie accused him. "Will you not dance any more?"

"I'm not fit for anything too vigorous," he said. "I can manage nothing more demanding than a nice sedate country dance."

It was possible he could manage a more vigorous dance, but he had attempted one too soon after his injury. His leg had given way and he'd tumbled over, right in the assembly room at the seaside town where they were staying, which had raised judgmental eyebrows and humiliating speculation that he was drunk. Since then, he'd been wary of attempting the livelier dances.

But he didn't mind admitting that now. How careful he had been before, to hide his weakness from the Misses Babworth, wanting to impress them and protect his own image. He'd never had to hide his weak leg from Sylvia; it was nothing but foolish vanity to try to hide it from anyone else.

"Those are dances for old people," Miss Lettie groaned with a roll of her eyes. "They're so boring!"

Prudence was frowning. "What do you mean, not fit for it?"

"A weak leg. It's better I rest it."

"Have you hurt yourself? You poor thing!" She boldly patted his forearm. "You should've told us. We could've looked after you."

"No need. It's permanent. An old injury."

As one, the two sisters' expressions changed, sinking into something like dismay. They exchanged a puzzled look and then frowned at him some more.

"I have a gammy leg," he said clearly. "For the most part, it isn't so bad, but I have limits."

"He broke his leg when he was in the Navy," Emily volunteered. "He used a cane when he first came to live with us, but he's so much better now. Do you remember that summer we went to the seaside? You swam for hours every day, and by the end of it, you were running up and down stairs like a child."

"I don't understand." Miss Lettie screwed up her face. "You mean you're … lame?"

"Miss Lettie, please," Cassandra scolded sharply.

Embarrassed annoyance rose in Isaac, further heightened as the two sisters shared a knowing look.

Emily nudged Lettie's shoulder. "Hardly! So he has a bad leg. It doesn't matter."

"As we've seen," Jane Newell pointed out, in her calm, sensible way. "He climbed that tree to get the mistletoe."

Miss Lettie scoffed. "What's the point of climbing a tree if one cannot dance a reel or fast quadrille?"

Miss Babworth was still eyeing his legs as if they had issued her a personal insult. "But you seem so… I mean, you don't look old and infirm."

"I'm not old or infirm," he said irritably. "Though I suppose I shall be one day, if I'm fortunate enough to live that long. As shall we all, and neither age nor infirmity lessens our worth as people."

His sharp admonishment did nothing to diminish the sisters' look of distaste, which they tried to cover with matching insincere smiles, before they turned and darted away, arm in arm. Isaac caught Miss Babworth saying something like "Old Whimper" and Miss Lettie responding with a squeal of disgust.

Interesting. Definitely a mistake to hide his injury from Miss Babworth out of misplaced pride, even when he thought he might court her—especially then. Marrying someone under false pretenses would be a mistake.

Yet another unexpected lesson from Sylvia.

"Oh, Isaac, I am sorry," Cassandra said. "They were terribly rude."

"I don't mind," he said honestly. "The flaw is theirs, not mine. 'Tis better to know their characters, I think."

Joshua barreled up to them, looked satisfied with the chaos he had caused. Past him, Sylvia, pink-cheeked, was laughing with another couple as they headed for the refreshments table. Emily and Jane trotted after her.

"Whose characters?" Joshua demanded.

"The Babworth sisters," Isaac said. "They've discovered I have a gammy leg and they're very unimpressed. My reluctance to dance a fast quadrille has lowered me considerably in their estimation."

"The hide of them!" Joshua said. "I'll show them a fast quadrille."

The threat made no sense, but Isaac appreciated the sentiment.

"But I do enjoy the slower dances," he said. "Cassandra, perhaps you might join me in a more sedate dance, if you can tolerate a partner who is old and infirm?"

Joshua glared at him. "Get your own bloody wife to dance with."

"All in good time."

"Not two months ago, you were blathering on about how much you wanted to get settled," Joshua reminded him. "Wanted a wife. Hated that your house was empty."

"Bed was empty too."

"*Was* empty?" Joshua's eyes narrowed. "Have you filled it? Is there someone sitting alone in your townhouse waiting for you?"

"No, no, no," Isaac said happily, waving a hand.

Another dance was starting—the waltz—and there was Lord Hardbury, honoring his word by leading Sylvia onto the floor, though she was looking mildly terrified. Isaac's chest swelled with affection for Hardbury and for every soul under this roof. An excellent ball, truly, with the extra coziness of being among friends and music and festivities when it was dark and cold outside.

He must go to more assemblies in Birmingham, he decided.

Had Sylvia attended assemblies in Birmingham? How odd to think they'd been living in the same city for a couple of years, though of course, given the hardships she'd suffered since her husband's death, she would not have been out dancing.

But she was dancing tonight. And she would dance at assemblies after she married, he supposed, dancing with her husband in that blue-green gown. Her future husband who owned a manor and, if the man had any sense, would dance with his wife every chance he got.

A drink, Isaac thought. What he needed right now was definitely a drink.

"You haven't courted anyone," Joshua said. "You said you wanted a wife. You asked about Miss Babworth's dowry."

"It's so bloody complicated," Isaac grumbled. "I

thought I liked Miss Babworth, but it seems she's one of those people who's at her best when things are going her way, and petty and spiteful when they're not."

A narrow escape, indeed.

"It's not like going shopping, is it?" he mused. "I can't just choose an appealing woman and install her in my house like a piece of furniture and expect everything to work out smoothly."

There were so many things to consider when choosing a spouse. What a decision. It was overwhelming. But no. He calmed himself. No need to rush in. His affair with Sylvia had removed the sense of urgency; that suggested he'd only been looking for a woman in his bed.

"How am I even to know if a woman will suit me?" he asked, almost to himself.

Joshua turned unusually pensive. "Perhaps the trick is to first know yourself and what truly matters to you. Then you'll not be blinded by false wishes and fears."

He didn't look at Cassandra, but Isaac saw him loop his fingers through hers, saw her squeeze his hand in response.

Isaac looked back across the milling ballroom: the couples, the singles, the groups. Perhaps he wasn't ready for marriage after all. His relationship with Sylvia felt so effortless; even when they disagreed, they easily put things right. But that was surely because they felt no pressure. Each knew the other was not a candidate for marriage, so they needn't worry about the future.

He could take his time. Go to more assemblies and dinners. After all, he wanted to be sure he chose a wife who accepted him as he was, gammy leg and all. A wife he could talk to, a wife he could have as a partner.

And, thanks to Sylvia, he need not rush into marriage until he found the right woman to suit.

CHAPTER 18

It was with a light head that Sylvia bid the rest of their party good night after they returned from the ball, and with tired legs that she climbed the stairs to her chamber.

"Good heavens," she said to Isaac, who followed a few steps behind. "My head feels as if I've drunk three pots of coffee and a quart of champagne, though I've had little but lemonade all night."

She sighed happily. What a magical night it had been.

"Thank you so much," she said. "Filling my dance card was such a lovely thing to do, for I should never have achieved that on my own. To think I attended a marchioness's ball and danced every set!" She whirled about on the stairs to face him and almost fell. He steadied her with his hands around her waist. "I waltzed with a marquess at a moonlit midwinter ball," she informed him earnestly. "When I'm one hundred years old, I'll still be boring everyone with the tale of this night. But he was ever so agreeable. He's very tall, much taller than you, which made me feel very short, but twice he remarked that I danced very nicely."

"Twice!" Isaac teased. "He must think you the finest dancer in all of England."

"More likely, he had run out of conversation and was racking his brains for something to say to this obscure little widow he found himself partnered with, but I don't mind."

Their faces were almost level, thanks to the stairs. Oh, how she wanted to melt into him. It was difficult, sometimes, to keep her distance in public. How lovely if she didn't have to pretend that Isaac was nothing more than her friend's daughter's husband's brother.

His hands tightened on her waist. His mouth twitched, once, twice, three times, and then he broke into that smile and everything inside her hummed in response.

Sylvia spun around and continued up the stairs.

These feelings, how intense they had become. She'd been throwing herself into other activities—working with Lady Charles in the still room, sewing her ballgown with Cassandra, playing with the babies, and the dogs, and the cat, even acting a role in one of Emily Lightwell's plays. Yet even when her thoughts were not actively on Isaac, recalling his words, his touch, their moments together— even then, his very existence had kindled a warmth that glowed inside her.

She knew what this feeling was called. She hardly dared name it, because she wasn't allowed to feel that for Isaac, not when she was engaged to someone else, not when her lover intended to take what he had learned from her and apply it to the fresh-faced young lady he would choose as his bride. Not when they were indulging in an affair that could be over before the next fall of snow.

Heartbreak was looming, the pain approaching like a runaway horse, and she could not stop it before it trampled her underfoot. She had never meant to fall in love, not with a charming, dashing younger man whom she could never have.

Yet her legs paused again, near the top of the stairs. Her heart lurched into a belated waltz of its own. Her knees trembled. Her breath grew short.

Turning back, she blurted out, "Are you still content with our arrangement?"

Perhaps his feelings have changed too, came a hopeful whisper inside. *Perhaps he too wants more than an affair. Perhaps…*

He blinked. "Immensely. Are you not?"

"Of course. I merely wanted to be sure. That is, we should say … if anything had changed. In what we wanted. From each other."

He glanced around: no witnesses.

"If you worry that I'm growing tired of you, Sylvia, I assure you that's not the case." He took her hands. "You've given me everything I wished for and a great deal I never even knew to wish for. You wanted to feel young, to gather joyous memories. If you're not satisfied, only tell me what more I can do, and I'll move heaven and earth to grant your every wish for the next week or two before we part."

"So nothing has changed for you?" she ventured, knowing the question was futile before the words were even out. *Before we part*, he had said, without so much as a flicker in those beautiful, expressive eyes.

"Everything has changed," he said. Her foolish heart leaped until he added, "You've been a great friend to me and shown me a whole new world. I'll remain ever grateful to you. Is something amiss?"

"No. Of course not."

Gratitude. What a feeling to inspire in a man. Hardly the passionate declaration a besotted woman wished to hear.

"As I said, I merely wished to make sure that we are still in accord."

Fool, she scolded herself, turning away, only to trip, whether from distraction or fatigue. Her shin banged against the riser of the top step. She stumbled. Somehow, Isaac moved from behind her, fast enough and strong enough to catch her before she fell too hard, so they ended up sprawled on the top step together.

She laugh-groaned at the throbbing pain in her shin. Isaac slipped an arm around her, his expression a mix of amusement and concern.

Oh, how his beloved face warmed her. She would hold onto the good feelings and make more memories and worry about the imminent shattering of her heart on some future day. She had years to feel miserable without him, and only a week or so to feel joy. She loved him; that was all. It was too late to stop that, so she wouldn't even bother to try. It was unlikely she'd ever love again, so this was not a feeling to squander.

"A bit too much punch tonight after all, my little teal duck?" Isaac teased gently.

"Not nearly enough, perhaps. But I danced all night, if you recall, and the exertion has turned my poor legs to jelly."

He ran a hand up one of her legs. "Was it this leg? Where did you hurt yourself? Shall I kiss it better?"

"Isaac!" She brushed him away. "Not out here. Someone might see."

"Then I'll kiss it better where no one can see."

Before she could guess his intention, he scooped her up into his arms. She hastily smothered her shrieks of delight.

"What are you doing?" she asked, even as she looped her hands around his neck.

"I'm rescuing the damsel in distress because I'm very gallant and noble."

"Are you really gallant and noble?"

He leered playfully. "Until I get you to your bed. At which point your gallant, noble knight will magically transform into a wicked, lustful rake."

"By the same magic, I suppose, the damsel in distress will turn into a brazen, wanton widow."

"I hope so. Bedroom magic is the best magic."

He shouldered into her room and laid her gently on the bed. Despite his teasing, he did not turn wicked and lustful—just as well, for she was so tired she doubted she could manage brazen or wanton tonight.

Instead, he slid her skirts up her calves, his fingers trailing over the stockings, seeking her bruised shin.

"I'm fine," she protested. "It's just a bump."

"Hush. A full inspection is required."

He eased off her slippers and tossed them over his shoulder. She sat up in protest.

"You mustn't," she said. "I've been dancing all night and my feet aren't clean."

He was undeterred. "Then I shall have to wash them."

"Isaac—"

"Sylvia. I spent fourteen years living in close quarters with dozens of unwashed sailors for weeks on end. Do you really think I'd be put off by a pretty lady's post-waltz toes?"

With a prosaicness she found more heart-warming than a million waltzes with aristocrats, Isaac shucked off his coat and set about untying and rolling down her stockings. Those, too, he tossed aside. He soaked a cloth in water from the pitcher and wrapped it over her hot, aching feet.

"Oh, that feels good," she moaned at its welcome

146

coolness, and groaned again when he pressed a thumb hard into the ball of her foot.

"Oh, sweet heaven, yes," she breathed.

"Good?"

"Heavenly. Do that again. More."

He obeyed. Again she moaned.

"I think you like that more than tupping," he said.

"So much more," she said, and laughed at his wounded expression. "I'm sure that with a mere touch to another part of my body, you'll easily change my mind, but right now, this is perfect."

He set to kneading the soles of her feet, and then her calves. Once she was a molten ball of bliss, he tidied her skirts, then stretched out alongside her. She snuggled against his chest, sighing as he planted a kiss on her head.

"This is very nice," she murmured. "You don't have to stay."

"Are you telling me to go?"

She reminded herself to speak plainly for him. "No. I like very much that you're here. But I'm too tired for anything more energetic than this."

"I find this very nice too," he said. "Such are the wonderful things you're teaching me."

No wonder he was *grateful* to her. The bitter thought stung her like a wasp. She hastily swatted it away. Foolish little duck.

She turned her senses simply to enjoying his solid body against hers. Their arrangement had given her everything she had asked for. She must not complain.

"I'm still so overexcited from the ball that despite how tired my body is, my mind won't sleep," she said.

"You've a book here. Shall I read to you?" She didn't move or open her eyes as he shifted to reach for the book on the bedside table. "What are you reading?"

"'Tis a Gothic novel," she confessed. "Poor Seraphina has been kidnapped by her sweetheart's evil brother, who has locked her in a bleak, windswept tower. Her only company is a white dove that comes to the window every day. Poor Seraphina is dreadfully overwrought. She spent several pages fainting and weeping, but she's since rallied, as every plucky heroine must, and has turned her thoughts to escape." She laughed. "I doubt it's to your taste."

"On the contrary. I find myself wild with desperation to know how our poor Seraphina will escape. Perhaps the dove will guide her to a secret passageway."

"Or carry a message for her, if the author conveniently forgets the tower room is bare and makes a writing desk appear on the next page."

"Or Seraphina will give the dove her garter to carry to her lover."

"Really, Isaac. It's not that sort of book."

He chuckled, and she snuggled against him contentedly. The sharp edges of her overexcited mind began to soften. Paper rustled somewhere above her head, but Isaac remained silent.

"Isaac," she murmured after a while, "I'll be able to hear you better if you read out loud."

The only sound in response was the rustling of paper. It slowly dawned on Sylvia, tired as she was, that it was not the sound of a book's page turning, but of a loose sheet of foolscap.

Then Isaac read out loud: "*I am troubled by a red itchy patch on my arm about the size of a penny. None of the lotions provides relief. First, I tried the lavender one, at intervals of two and a half hours, though my man neglected to remind me one day and nearly three hours passed between applications.*" Bloody hell. What is this?" he asked.

"A letter from Graham." Her voice was hoarse. She

had forgotten she'd used the letter to mark her place in the book.

Paper rustled again. "'*My digestion has improved thanks to Mrs. Yates's thin soups. She is kind enough to sit with me with her sewing in the evening, which reduces the cost of heating. I hope you will prove as frugal.*' Who is Mrs. Yates?"

"The housekeeper."

"Very cozy. Meanwhile, my toenails have turned green, so I soak them in mushroom soup for two and a half minutes each day while standing on my head."

"He did not write that."

"No more absurd than the rest of this drivel."

She sat up and snatched the letter away from him, suddenly wide awake. There was another page, on which she was drafting a reply and had crossed out several attempts. Had Isaac seen that too? Probably.

"I knew this man is older than you," Isaac said, in a flat and distant voice. "I didn't realize he's a frail octogenarian."

"He's barely forty. But he…"

"He's poorly?" he added, more kindly. "He truly is ill?"

Sylvia folded the letter so she didn't have to look at it.

"Not ill as such," she said carefully. "Overall, he appears very robust, but he seems to suffer from multiple ailments and he—"

"And he enjoys his many ailments very much," Isaac finished for her. "You will indulge him and listen to his complaints and cook possets and distill cordials, none of which will do any good but neither will they do any harm."

"We all have our weaknesses and flaws," she said stiffly, cheeks hot, spine chilled. "One letter cannot tell you enough."

"That one letter tells me a remarkable amount. He doesn't want a wife; he wants a nursemaid. I suppose marrying a nursemaid instead of hiring one is more frugal, not to mention permanent. After all, a nurse can leave her position. A wife must not. No wonder you came looking for me. I doubt he'll prove very entertaining in bed."

"Stop it," she snapped. "Don't mock him. To mock him is to mock my choices."

He rolled off the bed and landed on the floor with a thump. "But Sylvia. You must see. That man is ridiculous."

She rolled off the bed too, her bare feet digging into the soft rug as she faced him across the rumpled blankets.

"Is this the life you'll lead?" Isaac continued. "Shackled to this…" He gestured wildly at the letters clutched in her hand. "He already treats you as his employee. That entire letter was about him and what he needs. He didn't ask after you once. He can't even give you the courtesy of a 'how was your day?'"

"But he can give me security and stability. Yes, I'll tend to his ailments and soothe his complaints, and in return I'll have a roof over my head and food on my table. And let me tell you, it will be a relief, no— It will be sheer *bliss* if my only worry is whether I've put the right amount of honey in my husband's cordial or how to wash his nightshirts so the fabric doesn't itch. Such *ridiculous* problems are more appealing than the problem of keeping myself clothed and fed and off the street." She tossed the crumbled twist of letters aside. "I've become shallow and grasping and mercenary, you see. I've tried poverty, Isaac. I've tried getting through life with no family and mere pennies to live on and all my energy expended on thinking just one day ahead. Do you know what will be nicer than a 'how was your day'? Knowing I can think years ahead. That is luxury to me, and it is worth the price I must pay."

She marched around the bed toward him, stunned by the strength of her own reaction. He seemed stunned too, standing tall and straight, with his shirt half undone, his fists clenched, his eyes roaming wildly over her face. Yet his expression still betrayed his distaste.

He had betrayed her. Yes, that was the word. Betrayed her by failing to understand her motives. By making her feel ashamed of choosing to marry a man she didn't respect, by making her feel small and weak for having failed somehow. How dare he let her down! And how dare she even accuse him of that, for he had broken no promises and she had no right to ask for anything more.

To think she had risked her safe future with Graham for—what? For the passing pleasures of the flesh. *That* was what was ridiculous: falling in love with Isaac. How despicable she was, how reckless, immoral, weak.

The bitter emotions burned like acid; they had nowhere to go but into her words. She rounded on him, wanting to shove him and shake him and she knew not what.

He stood like a disheveled centurion, solid and still in the face of her advance, but glaring at her through the strands of hair tumbling over his face.

"Don't you *dare* judge my choices, because I don't have a lot of them," she said through her tight, quivering mouth. "I've betrayed him, and I gave myself a nice excuse to do so, but I'll be a good, loyal wife, because never again will I let myself forget what he's giving me, what I have no other way of getting. It won't be an exciting life, but excitement is not to be recommended."

"You found me exciting," he said.

"You are excitement and diversion. I need safety and stability. This interlude—"

"No."

The word dropped into the room with the heaviness of

an iron bar. It seemed he already knew what she was going to say. But she had to say it.

"This interlude has gone as far as it can," she said firmly. "Our affair has achieved its aim. You know enough to please your future wife in bed, and I have enjoyed my torrid affair and now I can settle down."

"That's it, then?" He seemed taken aback, as if he'd never imagined this could happen. That lost, vulnerable look she hadn't seen in days drifted into his beautiful, expressive eyes. "No more of this? No more of…"

Her heart ached. But her wounded heart and his wounded pride were irrelevant here. They had enjoyed a pretty fantasy, but reality had not changed.

"'Tis time you returned to seeking a wife," she said. "I've nothing more to teach you."

He scoffed. "I read your letter and made you angry so you punish me by ending the affair."

"I'm not punishing you. The affair was always going to end, by its very definition. The letter is merely a reminder that we have real lives outside this foolish fantasy, and our liaison was nothing more than a pleasant interlude, to make each of us ready for marriage to someone else."

And yet.

She knew what she wanted from him; perhaps one final attempt?

"You can't deny me marriage to someone else, for you're surely not thinking of marrying me yourself."

"Well, no. This was never— And you're not—"

He stopped short, then cursed and raked his fingers through his hair. But the words had been said.

"Precisely." Her voice was small but unwavering. "This was never, and I am not."

Not *what* didn't need to be said. She was not young. She was not suitable. She was not dowered. She was not a good bride for a man of twenty-seven just finding his way in the world. They were at different stages of their lives.

"But to Graham Ossett, I *am*." She hugged herself, shivering in her lovely ballgown. "I am no fool, Isaac. The way you mock my choices proves you don't understand them. Or perhaps I am a fool, to have risked a safe, comfortable future for a charming young man who sees the world very differently to me."

Shaking his head, he stepped toward her. Longing coursed through her again. She steeled herself, willed herself to resist this temptation.

Temptation was where it began. She mustn't surrender to temptation again. It had been truly unfair to dismiss Isaac as all spicy steam and no pudding, because he was definitely plum pudding, warm, spicy, sweet, and very, *very* substantial. But plum pudding was a special treat; it was eaten only once a year, and then it was gone. Graham was as tasty and exciting as a stale oatcake, but he would last.

"But Sylvia, you can't think you'll be happy with him."

"Oh, Isaac, for the first time I feel the years between us. Happiness is a luxury not all of us can afford." Acid tears stung her eyes. "You've given me what I needed, and I hope I've done the same for you. But if this discussion has shown us anything, it's that we best end this now."

She swiped at the tears, as his eyes shadowed with hurt. But before she could read anything more into his expression, he nodded, swept up his coat, and disappeared out the door.

CHAPTER 19

The new year was not yet a full day old and already Isaac hated it.

A restless fury burned, making his back muscles tense and his hands clench into fists and his legs kick things as he roamed through the house.

How could she? How could Sylvia, with her generous spirit and gentle humor and industrious energy, sacrifice herself to some whining old man? True, forty was not old in years, but some people were ancient at fifteen, and not in the calm, wise way, but in the rigid, peevish way. The man couldn't help it if he was truly poorly, but he could help being peevish and petty and self-absorbed.

And she—she meant to marry him! How *could* she?

Somehow, he wound up in the library. Perhaps he'd find a copy of that novel she was reading; he wanted to ask Sylvia how poor Seraphina escaped, which was a stupid thing to ask anyone, let alone the young widow who had just kicked him out of her bed.

He didn't even know what he was looking for until he

found a shelf of books about the middle of England. More specifically, a book on country houses.

Worcestershire, he thought. What was the place name? Kemble Manor, that was it. Graham Ossett of Kemble Manor. Ossett, like an ossuary, a place where they stored human bones. Sounded about right.

Dust puffed around him as he opened the enormous book and flipped over the big pages. The grandest houses earned color plates and lengthy descriptions, from extensive family histories to the dimensions of the rooms. More modest houses had line sketches and a few paragraphs. Minor houses had a mere paragraph of text. It was very satisfying to discover that Kemble Manor merited no picture and only ten—no, nine lines. Ha! *So much for your grandeur, Graham Ossett of Kemble Manor. You do not have such a grand country estate after all.*

Still, it was grander than Isaac's country estate, given that Isaac didn't own a country estate and quite possibly never would.

Sylvia didn't even care for country life, particularly. But she would learn to, he supposed. Because she was practical and resourceful, and she did what was needed to survive.

The door opened. The inventors came in. Isaac guiltily shoved the book back on the shelf and grabbed another. Better no one guess at his absurd new obsession with Sylvia's intended. He tried to summon up some guilt and outrage for what he and Sylvia had done to the man but found he could not, not now he had the fellow's measure. Besides, he had seen the letter she'd been writing in response—trying to write, anyway. A letter designed to please. A letter written out of desperation and duty. Like a job.

He swiped dust off the book and flipped through the

pages, pretending to read so no one would come near. He didn't see a thing on the pages, until his eye was caught by a pressed flower, placed there by Cassandra or one of her sisters as a girl and forgotten about over time. Drying herself out like a pressed flower: That was what Sylvia would be doing to herself if she married that man. In a few years, she would look like a flower still, but she'd be dry and papery, like the book, like old bones, like the peevish self-absorbed man

He slammed the book shut and shoved it back on the shelf. He spun around and was almost at the door when again it opened.

Sylvia stood there. His heart leaped, and he almost rushed at her, desperate for her smile.

But when she saw him, her expression turned stiff.

"Mr. Isaac," she said coolly.

He remembered, suddenly, her worn, pinched look when she first arrived at Sunne Park. Now she had new plumpness to her form and color in her cheeks and brightness in her eyes. *I helped give her that*, he thought proudly. Graham Bloody Ossett wouldn't give her that. The man wouldn't notice the color in her cheeks, or if she was tired or worried; he'd be too concerned with his own made-up ailments. Isaac had given her what she needed. And she had cut him off! Ended the affair!

"You're right, it's none of my business," he said harshly. "If you want to marry some whining, self-centered hypochondriac, it's all the same to me. If you want to bury yourself in some dusty old manor until you dry up into a thin, colorless, papery version of yourself, well, why should I give a damn?"

Her jaw tensed. "No reason for you to care," she agreed thinly, "if you don't understand why I might make that choice or what I need." She glanced past him. He was blocking her path. "Were there any other enlightening views you wished to share, Mr. Isaac, or might I be given some peace to enjoy my day?"

Guilt fumbled through him then, chased away by another burst of rage and shame. She moved past him before he could say he was sorry, he didn't know what he was saying, he wasn't angry, not really, he just needed to escape into the garden and breathe in the icy air.

THE NEXT DAY, Isaac was relieved to ride over to Vindale Court to call on Lord Hardbury about the assignment he owed in exchange for Hardbury's waltz. It was a complex matter that ate up several hours, and how good it felt to lose himself entirely in some unknown party's nefarious deeds.

Back at Sunne Park, he was informed that tea was being served, so he headed into the drawing room, only to stop short. Because the clumsy bloody footman had not had the sense to warn him that it was Sylvia serving the tea. Not Cassandra or Lady Charles, who were preoccupied with little Charlie and baby Rose. No, it was Sylvia with the teapot in hand, sitting straight-backed to pour. She looked poised and relaxed and completely at home.

She looked like she was already the bloody lady of the stupid bloody manor.

"Are you aware you've stopped under a kissing bough, Mr. Isaac?" came Miss Lettie Babworth's sly sing-song voice.

Isaac glanced up and cursed, just as Miss Prudence Babworth planted herself before him.

"Mr. Isaac, I'm sorry for what I said at the ball," she said in a small voice.

He stared at her stonily, hardly seeing her, all his awareness on Sylvia and the clink and tinkle of porcelain plates and silver spoons. What the hell was Miss Babworth even babbling about?

She glanced up at the kissing bough, then offered him a shy smile. "Look, there's still a berry left. One kiss remains."

"Bloody hell, enough of these stupid bloody kisses," he snarled, and he picked that stupid ugly berry and threw it at the wall with a splat, then turned his back on the ladies' stunned silence and stomped out of the room.

Joshua found him in the nursery, sitting on the floor beside the dollhouse, cutting and stitching enough miniature blankets to smother a whole city of dolls.

"What the blazes is wrong with you?" he asked.

Isaac ignored him.

"You're not still sulking over what those idiot girls said?"

He lifted his head. "What the hell are you talking about?"

"The Babworth sisters."

"What about them?"

Joshua tumbled onto the floor beside him. "Cassandra got the full story. Some village they lived in, the schoolmaster or vicar or someone was a nasty old stinker with a gammy leg. Used to limp through town throwing stones at their dog and trying to whack them with his walking stick. Old Whimper they called him—Mr. Wimpole or something his name was. So now they're prejudiced against men with bad legs. Cassandra pointed out that Old Whimper was cruel because of his character, not his leg, and they were chastened and promised to apologize."

"Oh. Yes. Miss Babworth did apologize, I suppose."

"Right before you threw a mistletoe berry at her head."

"I didn't throw it at her head. I threw it at the wall. If I'd thrown it at her head, she'd be wearing mistletoe jam on her face."

He turned his attention back to the blankets.

Joshua watched him a while. "Isaac, are you all right?"

"Just sick of the stupid bloody countryside," he said.

Eventually, Joshua just nodded and asked if the dolls needed tablecloths too. This led to a discussion of different types of tables, and by the time Cassandra found them, an hour later, they were designing a miniature roulette table for the dolls.

ON THE THIRD day after Sylvia ended the affair, Isaac avoided everyone all day. He had no choice but to dress for the evening, though, as the residents of Vindale Court and other neighbors were joining them for dinner.

From his seat, he watched Sylvia down the table. He indulged fantasies of marching down the room, tossing her over his shoulder, and carrying her away. Or fantasies of her meeting his eyes and smiling with that gentle, teasing humor, then coming close to kiss him and say she was sorry and she forgave him and everything would be all right.

But she didn't meet his eyes, except to shoot him a stern look that he understood to mean, "stop staring at me, people will notice."

On the bright side, the Babworth sisters were ignoring him. One of the dinner guests was a young squire called

Mr. Moffat, accompanied by his sister Miss Moffat, and Isaac was relieved that Prudence Babworth was more interested in them than in him.

It was no better in the drawing room later. The ladies were taking turns to play the pianoforte and sing. Sylvia played a little too, while Isaac sat next to Lady Charles, who offered him a plate of coffee creams and gently patted his hand.

"She ended it," he said, without looking at her.

"Such is the nature of affairs," she said softly. "You knew it would end."

"But I didn't know it would end *badly*."

"There's something you can do about that."

His head whipped around. "She wants to meet with me again? Did she say that to you?"

"No, Isaac." Lady Charles squeezed his hand. "I meant about the 'badly' part. 'Tis not too late to make your parting amicable."

Across the room, Sylvia finished playing, then she stood to turn the pages for Jane Newell. Watching her, Isaac's stomach muscles tightened, clenching inside him the way a shipwrecked man clenched a piece of wood. That made his chest tighten too, which made his chest ache. He tried to massage away that ache, that tightness, the way he massaged away the ache in his leg, but nothing would give him ease.

When Sylvia left the pianoforte, he edged his way around the room to stand at her side. She was as tense as a sail full stretched. She didn't look at him, but she didn't move away.

"Don't marry him," he said to her profile.

Her chin came up. She didn't turn. "I beg your pardon?"

"Don't marry him. Marry me."

Her gaze remained fixed on a point across the warm, candlelit room. Jane and Emily were singing a sweet duet about ringing bells and misty mornings. Under their tune hummed the others' amiable conversations. It all seemed to be happening in another world from where Isaac stood.

"Why?" she finally asked.

"He's ridiculous. He won't make you happy."

"Being happy is not my greatest concern."

"I can make it so you don't have to marry him."

A gentle sigh wafted between them. "I'm not a kitten stuck up a tree, Isaac," she said softly. "You like to be gallant, but I don't need to be rescued this time. Mr. Ossett already rescued me, you see."

"Did he really rescue you?" The words came pouring out of him with unfamiliar urgency. "Or did he see a chance to exploit your difficulties and force you into service? I see it now: the impoverished young widow eking out a living making cordials, the hypochondriac sampling her wares, the widow's empathy soothing him more than any balm, the hypochondriac noting her patched dress, her thin cheeks, her lack of family to protect her. Aha, says the hypochondriac— He won't just buy the cordials, he'll buy the woman who makes them too. *Did* he rescue you, Sylvia? Or did he prey on you? Because he sounds very predatory to me."

She swallowed hard. Her knuckles were white where she gripped her glass.

"Ah, so I'm not a kitten, but a poor little mouse to be pounced upon."

"Mice are clever and resourceful. But he could see you were in need and knew he could make you dependent on him."

She shook her head. "This is what you still fail to understand. I'll be dependent on whichever man I marry, yet marrying is the best way to ensure I don't become dependent on the workhouse. Perhaps he preyed on me, but he could only do that because he truly understands what I need."

"Then take me. Don't marry him just because you're grateful to him."

She faced him then. Something fierce burned in her gaze. "As you are grateful to me?"

"Of course I'm grateful, but that's... I can look after you, if that's your concern. I'm not wealthy, and we'd have to be careful, but I earn enough to support a wife. I mean, I'm not fancy enough to have a country estate but—"

"Stop it. This isn't helping. That's not what I want."

"You mean, I'm not what you want."

With a sigh, she closed her eyes. When she opened them, she was again giving him her profile, letting him see the shape of her lips as she sipped her drink, the pulse in her throat as she swallowed. He could not believe he had lost the right to kiss those lips, that pulse, and he didn't understand why.

Still she didn't look at him as she spoke. "I fear that, despite everything, you don't really see what I need."

"Didn't I give you what you wanted? Memories and excitement and youth?"

"And it was diverting and wonderful." She sounded sad, though. "But we both know it wasn't real. Was it? It wasn't something that mattered in the real world."

"Right. Not real. Didn't matter."

Around them, the fire was crackling, the ladies were singing, the gentlemen were laughing, and all Isaac could hear was a roaring in his head, like the turbulent ocean on a stormy day.

He had proposed to her. She had turned him down. Yet still he couldn't move away.

"Is this what happens, with affairs?" he asked. "Is this how they always go?"

"I don't know. I've never had one before. I never will again."

"Then it was only me."

Her lips curved into a small smile he didn't understand. "Yes. It was only you."

THE FOLLOWING DAY, nothing was better. Isaac passed Sylvia in the hallway, but she looked right through him. The rejected marriage proposal followed him around like a jeering street performer. She could have spent every Christmas for the rest of her life at Sunne Park if she had said yes. He had offered her a lifeboat.

And she had turned him down.

The drawing room that evening became unbearable. Isaac escaped for the quiet of his room, but he reached the door just as she was coming in. She avoided his eyes, offered a mere bob of her head.

He could not bear it anymore.

"Mrs. Ray," he said.

She paused. "Mr. Isaac."

"The things I've said these past days," he started.

Finally, her gaze snapped to his. He read distress in her eyes. That ache squeezed his chest again. He fought to catch his breath.

"Please accept my apologies for upsetting and offending you."

She extended a hand as if to take his arm, but withdrew it again without touching him. He wanted to hold her. He could not. She was not his to hold. Never had been.

"Accepted. But let's not confuse our time together for anything other than what it was."

"But what was it?" he whispered hoarsely as she moved past him.

If she heard him, she did not reply.

CHAPTER 20

By Twelfth Night, the kissing boughs were denuded of berries and their candles were little more than ragged stubs. The garlands that Sylvia and the other ladies had sewn and hung on Christmas Eve were sagging wearily, and the greenery around the house was brittle and dry.

Sylvia wasn't sure how much more she could bear. She craved Isaac with a relentless hunger that stunned her; every futile encounter tore pieces off her heart. But an impulsive proposal was not enough. And as for his summary of Graham? Well, he'd not said anything she hadn't already known.

But here was what Isaac failed to see: She and Graham understood each other. Graham might not care about her day-to-day well-being, but he understood the fear and need that drove her. And how dare Isaac suggest Graham had preyed upon her! How dare he paint her as helpless and weak! She knew exactly what she was getting; her very actions to save herself demanded every ounce of her strength.

Isaac's proposal had been misguided, fueled by guilt,

gallantry, gratitude, a promise she could not trust. All he offered was an impulsive marriage to a man who was at a different stage of life to her and didn't know what he wanted. She longed to be with him, but not like that. But how else could she explain it? *The clues lie everywhere, if one chooses to see,* he had told her, proud of his investigative skills. Yet all the clues were there, and still he did not see.

Isaac hadn't understood her, after all.

So she had struggled to avoid him, struggled to immerse herself in every household activity she could find, and then enjoy the Twelfth Night festivities, as the household laid the Christmas season to rest.

Mercifully, Sylvia was seated at the other end of the table from Isaac for the Twelfth Night dinner. Less mercifully, they were seated on opposite sides, so when she looked down the length of the table, as it seemed she too often did, all she saw was him: flirting, chatting, smiling. If he gave her so much as a fleeting thought, he didn't betray it with so much as a fleeting glance.

Well. Her rejection of his proposal had soothed him, perhaps. He had tried to rescue her, she had refused his help, and now his conscience was clear.

Like everyone else, she oohed and aahed over the enormous, elaborate cake. With a pang of homesickness, she thought of the patisseries in Birmingham, whose windows would be lit up to show off their grand arrays of Twelfth Cakes. She shoved her longing for the city aside— it was the country life for her now—and exchanged pleasant comments with the gentleman seated to her left. He was a young squire called Mr. Moffat, whom Sylvia recalled as the farmer with the cows whom Prudence Babworth had so admired before her head was turned by dashing Isaac DeWitt.

While everyone was eating their fruit cake and

speculating about who would find the bean and pea in their slice, and so be named king and queen, Sylvia merely poked and prodded, crumbling it with her fork. She hardly knew what Mr. Moffat was about when he slapped the table so hard the dishes rattled, and cried, "I say, Mrs. Ray! You've got the pea in your cake! You're to be our queen!"

Cheers went up, along with applause, and those seated around her craned their necks to see. Sylvia focused her vision and there it was: a dried pea sitting in the detritus of her cake. She was to be the Twelfth Night Queen.

Oh dear. She was not in a very royal mood.

A cry rippled around the table: "Who has the bean in his cake? Who is the king?" And because every sin requires a punishment, Emily Lightwell yelled, "It's Isaac! Isaac's the king! And Mrs. Ray is his queen."

Sylvia's heart crumbled like her cake. Their eyes met. His gaze was forceful, relentless. In those expressive eyes, she read accusation and understanding and something like a demand. Her breath stopped, her chest tightened; that gaze held her until every part of her felt shivery and light.

The moment seemed to endure an eternity, but it could not have been even a minute, before Emily was brandishing a fur-lined cloak and ornate crown, made for one of her Shakespeare plays, saying, "Your Majesty, Queen Sylvia! You must wear your regal costume and take your place beside the king."

Mr. Moffat raced to help Sylvia push back her chair. Down the other end, Isaac stood too. Lady Charles was at her side, whispering, "Are you all right, dear?" but Sylvia barely managed to say "Yes, of course," before she was whisked away by Emily, while Isaac was corralled by Cassandra, and the two sisters herded them to each other's side. Emily tossed their royal cloaks around them and plonked their crowns haphazardly on their heads.

Isaac's royal red cloak was lopsided, as was his crown. They had helped each other dress so many times that their hands acted of their own accord. Without thinking, Sylvia reached out and arranged his cloak over his shoulders, and he shook out a crease in hers. She straightened his crown, and he pushed hers off her forehead. But his cloak wasn't quite right, and her hands were on his shoulders again, flipping over a piece of fur that was turned the wrong way up.

Their eyes met, so close this time. Close enough to kiss, to lean into each other, to become one. For a heartbeat, they were back in their cabin; the next heartbeat hurled them back to reality. They dropped their hands, jumped away, darted wild glances like a pair of thieves, but no one seemed to have witnessed their crime.

Emily, the self-appointed director of the household's Twelfth Night drama, looped their elbows and presented them to the group, who responded with a cheer. Isaac's arm was hot and heavy and strong against hers.

"What do we do as king and queen?" she asked. Her attempt at cheer made her voice too loud and bright. But no one noticed that either; drinks had flowed tonight.

"You must lead the procession to the bonfire," Emily announced. "You must give everyone orders."

"What orders?" Sylvia asked, but it didn't matter, because Emily was already issuing the orders herself.

Every household developed its own traditions. At Sunne Park, the tradition was for the king and queen to wait while everyone else ran about cutting down the bedraggled kissing boughs and gathering up every bit of Christmas greenery they could find. Laden with dead branches, jostling each other good-naturedly, they formed two lines behind Isaac and Sylvia, who shared a look at the absurdity of their situation.

"What are the chances?" he murmured.

"This is why I don't gamble."

"Would you call this a win or a loss?"

She had no words. His expression gentled.

"I have won much, but lost more," he said softly.

"Isaac—"

But there was no time to talk. Emily, having bossed everyone into tidy lines, claimed her place at the head of the procession. She played a flute as she led the way, kicking her legs out to the side and whirling around to dance backward. Sylvia glanced over her shoulder, to see the others mimicking Emily's funny walks and dance steps, bumping into each other with raucous laughter, as the chaotic procession stumbled out of the house.

Outside on the lawn, a huge bonfire was crackling cheerily under the dark sky, adorned with pinpricks of stars and the waning moon. Workers and villagers were already there, having been treated to their own generous feast.

Emily led Isaac and Sylvia to their "thrones," a pair of wing-backed chairs placed a comfortable distance from the flames, safe from the sweet, spiraling smoke and soaring ash. They were served mulled wine, which they had to take, sitting stiffly to watch as everyone hurled the dried greenery onto the bonfire and cheered as the flames leaped higher into the cold winter air.

A troupe of local musicians launched into a lively jig, filling the air with the sounds of their fiddles and flutes and drums. As if freed from the restraints of civilization, the dancing began, family members, guests, neighbors, workers, and tenants mingling freely on this night of all nights.

Sylvia could feel Isaac's gaze upon her. She turned to him. Light from the bonfire flickered over his face. Even under the absurd crown, his features were serious and strong, as if the last of his naivety was melting away.

"Would you like to dance?" he asked.

"Do they expect us to?"

"Who bloody well cares what they expect? Do you *want* to?"

"They've been so good to me; I don't want to——"

"Do you want to dance with me or not? That's not such a difficult question, I would've thought."

"You know it's not simple."

"I know nothing. That's what I know. Absolutely nothing. You promised to teach me, and all I've learned is that I know nothing at all. Nothing about anything." He grabbed her hand. "Sylvia, we——"

"I can't."

She tugged her hand free and stood, not knowing what to do or where to go.

He stood too.

"Dance with me," he said softly, so softly she felt the words rather than heard them. "Dance with me."

His hand was extended. She rested her palm on his. How easily and naturally she moved into his embrace. They kept enough distance to avoid comment, but his presence enveloped her all the same. The music was lively, the crowd chaotic, but Sylvia's legs would not move. Neither did his. Her gaze roamed hungrily over his features: the angles of his nose and cheekbones and jaw, the soft promise of his lips. *Remember this,* she thought. *Remember his face, in the firelight, under the stars on a clear winter's night.*

"You wanted something to remember," he said. "Will you remember me?"

"Always."

"I'll never forget you."

"We never forget our first."

"Not because you were my first, but because you are *you*. You changed my life, you changed me, you—"

Someone bumped into her. She stumbled into him. He caught her. Suddenly, his touch seared her as if she'd been hurled into the flames along with all the dried-up leaves. She bounced back away from him.

"I can't. Excuse me. Please."

She whirled away, the crown tumbling from her head. She let it fall as she ran toward the house, stumbling in the half-light, under the weight of the faux-royal cloak. Somehow she reached the conservatory, desperately joggling the handles to open the door as if it were the gateway to heaven and the hounds of hell were baying at her heels.

No bloodthirsty hounds: only Isaac, reaching past her to open the door, pulling her into the conservatory after him, spinning her to face him, and then claiming her with his arms, kissing her with a furious hunger she could not deny. She stretched as tall as she could, wrapped her arms around his neck, gripped his thick hair to press against him, to push herself into his searching, conquering mouth.

Her back hit a wall. His hands were shoving up her skirts; her hands were attacking his breeches. They'd never done this before, not like this, but they knew what to do. He lifted her up and onto him, her back against the wall, her legs circling him, his arms holding her up as he thrust into her. There was light enough for their eyes to meet, to communicate a thousand things they did not know how to put into words.

Then his crushingly frantic pace stopped. He moved slowly now, achingly slowly, moving their bodies together with an excruciating tenderness. His arms cradled her, held her steady, as close to each other as they could get.

"Is this what you meant, when you said what lay between us is mere diversion and not real?" he asked hoarsely, while he moved within her. "Is this why you said it didn't matter in the real world? Is that what you're feeling now? That you and me, we aren't real. You and me, we don't matter at all."

She didn't have the words, and nothing had changed, so she buried her face in the warm, spicy skin of his neck and held him tight and loved him with her body as she would never love anyone again.

CHAPTER 21

I saac couldn't sleep. Being the middle of winter, dawn took a hundred bloody years before it bothered to finally creep in, allowing him to escape from the cold solitude of his room into the cold expanse of the outdoors. For the most part, he was happy to be back on land, but sometimes he yearned for the ocean, for those perfect moments when the world was empty of everything but the wind and the water and the ship slicing through the waves.

She had left him in the conservatory after their bout the previous evening. "Don't follow me," she'd said, and so he hadn't, but all night he thought of her, just down the hall, while his mind relived their past and imagined their future a thousand different ways.

He walked and walked, his boots crunching across the frost and snow under the hostile, lightening sky. It was wretchedly cold and his leg ached, but he ignored the stupid thing. That sort of pain didn't matter. Not compared to the pain of Sylvia running away from him in the night. He walked for miles, ended up at a neighboring farmhouse. The neighbors fed him and entertained him, until he felt rested enough to walk all the way home.

Back in the house, he marched directly to the still room. She could not marry this parasite Ossett. Isaac wouldn't allow it. She wouldn't like him saying that, she would insist it was her choice not his, but he was ready to argue with that too.

Lady Charles was alone in the still room, singing to herself as she ground something using a mortar and pestle.

"Where is she?" he demanded.

She whirled around and stared at him blankly.

"Mrs. Ray," he said flatly. "Where is she? I must speak to her."

With a sigh, she lay down the pestle, wiped her hands, and crossed in front of him. She rubbed his upper arms up and down, as if warming a child. It did not warm him.

"Oh, Isaac. Sweetheart," she said.

"What?" He pulled away. "You speak as if she has died." He could not breathe. "Is she ill? Did something happen?"

Had he hurt her last night? The cold, the— No, she was robust. She had survived worse things than him. But if she—

"She was very well when she left. But you—"

"Left?" he repeated numbly.

The pitying kindness in her eyes made him want to scream. "She has borrowed a carriage and gone," Lady Charles explained. "She wished to take advantage of the clear roads, she said, to be sure she arrives in Worcestershire in time for her wedding. She decided to leave before the weather turned again."

He thumped the workbench so hard the pestle rolled onto the floor. "You should not have let her go."

"Would you have had me confine her to her room? Bind her to a chair and lock the door?"

"Yes, yes, and yes. Lock her in the tower like Seraphina."

"Who's Seraphina?"

He ignored the question, spun, and marched for the door.

"Isaac," Lady Charles called softly.

He stopped short, eyes on the doorway, on the cold, barren flagstones beyond, letting her talk to his back.

"I know it hurts," she said. "That's one of the hardest lessons to learn about love. The more wonderful love feels at its best, the more it hurts at its worst."

"Love," he repeated, hearing the bitter rue shading his own tone.

Of course. What a naive fool he was. Sylvia had promised to teach him everything, and she had. She had taught him how it felt to love, and she had taught him how he could destroy himself if he failed to see love for what it was and carelessly tossed it away.

"*I am grateful to you,*" he had said.

"*Do not marry me out of gratitude,*" she had said.

Grateful. How very, very misguided he had been, to have thought he felt friendship and gratitude, when what he felt was love. Ruined by his own bloody naivety.

Oh Sylvia, he thought. *This was the most important lesson of all. Why didn't you teach it to me plain, instead of leaving me alone to figure it out by myself?*

"I love her," he told the world, and the words felt right. "Does she love me? But why did she leave me for him? Because of his country estate?"

"Because sometimes love isn't enough," came the quiet reply. "Not if we can't give each other what we need."

THE BLASTED SKY was already starting to dim again. He had foolishly wasted the scarce hours of daylight traipsing around the countryside instead of locking Sylvia in her room until she agreed to stay. No matter. He barged into the stables anyway.

The groom refused him a horse, but he pushed past him, and the groom pushed back, until the stablemaster intervened. He refused Isaac a horse too. It was getting dark, the stablemaster pointed out, and it looked like the weather might turn again soon, and if Mr. Isaac wished to risk his neck, that was his own bloody business, but damned if the stablemaster would let him risk a horse too.

He was stuck. They wouldn't let him go after her, but he couldn't *not* go after her, so he stood there, mutinously facing off with the older man, until Joshua appeared and shoved him into an empty stall like a wayward horse.

"Lady Charles says you're upset about Mrs. Ray," Joshua said. "Says you had an affair with her. Says you're—"

"I'm losing her, Joshua." He pressed his hand into the rough wall to keep from falling over. "I just realized I love her, because I'm a stupid idiot, and now I'm going to lose her."

"I nearly lost Cassandra, something similar," Joshua said. "Nearly destroyed our marriage."

Isaac snorted. "I'm not surprised, the way you used to behave. You don't deserve her."

"I know. But I try to deserve her. Every day, I try. Pleasing her is what I live for now, and it's the best part of my life. So I understand if you—"

"You understand nothing."

Isaac tried to shove past him, but Joshua shoved back, blocking his escape.

"Damn you, move!" he snarled. "I have to go."

"Not now. It's getting dark and they say the weather might turn."

"That's why! Don't you see? That's why I must go after her now!" Isaac thumped the wall. "The weather will turn, the roads will become impassable, and then I won't reach her in time, and she'll be stuck there forever, in Kemble Mausoleum in Worse-shire, married to a pile of dead bones."

Once more, he surged forward. Once more, Joshua held him back.

"You're worrying my wife, and I get very upset when anyone worries my wife."

"Listen to me carefully, you numbskull." Isaac gave his brother's shoulder another shove for good measure. "Sylvia has left me to marry someone else. Some bony fellow. With a bloody skeleton."

"You can't fault him for having a skeleton. This Mr.— What's his name?"

"Ossuary."

Joshua cocked his head, distracted. "Isn't an ossuary a room made of human bones?"

"Precisely. I bet that's what his fancy country manor is built from: dry, dead human bones. She intends to marry him and I won't let her."

"Why not?"

"Because he's a predatory, parasitical hypochondriac who will treat her like his personal nursemaid. He'll take and take and give nothing in return until he gradually sucks her dry."

Joshua shrugged. "So you marry her then. Simple."

"I asked. She said no."

Cassandra bustled into the stall with them, pieces of straw clinging to the raised hem of her skirts. "Here you are, Isaac. Are we talking about Mrs. Ray? Mama said you're upset she's gone because you love her and want to marry her."

Joshua slid an arm around her waist. "Isaac asked Mrs. Ray to marry him, but she said no, and now she's run off to marry some skeleton who lives in a room made of human bones and will suckle her until she too is bone dry."

"That makes no sense."

"Of course not. Who wants to marry a skeleton?"

Cassandra gave an exasperated huff. "You two are the worst people on earth for a sensible discussion of love." Her expression softened as she took Isaac's hand. "She turned you down?"

Soul-deep weariness swept over him. "I told her she mustn't marry him because he'll treat her like a nursemaid, so she should marry me instead."

An embarrassed little silence tiptoed around them. Even Joshua looked embarrassed for him, and Joshua was almost impossible to embarrass.

Worse was the pity in Cassandra's voice when she said, very carefully, "*That* was how you proposed?"

Isaac groaned. "It was terrible, wasn't it? Then I told her I was grateful to her, and she told me not to marry her out of gratitude." He thrust his hands into his hair. "I didn't know," he went on, as if pleading for mercy from a black-capped hanging judge. "But maybe she loves me too? She doesn't love him. She knows what he is, but she's still marrying him and not me."

"She must have a reason," Cassandra said, very reasonably. "Perhaps she feels obliged to him?"

"He doesn't deserve it."

"Then why is she marrying him?"

He ignored the question. "I have to go after her. Now. Do you know how long the nights are? Last night—" He shook his head. "Last night was the longest night of my life."

"Technically," Joshua said, "the longest night would have been about two weeks ago."

Isaac glared at him. "The longest night of my life," he repeated through gritted teeth. "And you want me to do it again tonight?"

"Technically, tonight will be shorter than last night. Only by about a few minutes or so but—"

With a roar, he shoved past his brother like a maddened bull and burst out of the dim, dusty stables, gulping down the crisp air of the darkening day.

Before him rose Sunne Park, the jumbled, rambling house outlined against the purple-gray sky. The first candles and fires glowed in the windows, as the first stars appeared amid the gathering clouds.

Those bloody clouds were ruining his life.

A hand landed on his shoulder: Joshua, quiet for once, standing by his side. Another hand squeezed his other arm: Cassandra. The pair of them flanking him. By his side and on his side, whatever foolish things he did.

Sylvia had no one in her life like that. No one but him.

"To make her marry you and not him," Joshua finally said, "you must understand why she's choosing him."

"If you love each other, that's an excellent foundation," Cassandra added. "Can you give her what she needs?"

I need security, she had said.

When she was younger, she had wanted excitement, but now she wanted reliability.

To mock him is to mock my choices.

The man owned a country estate. Isaac would never own a country estate.

He scowled up at Sunne Park. Its very presence seemed to mock him. Sunne Park was grand enough to merit a color plate in the book on country houses. It even merited a history of the first owners, who had built it three centuries before. It would likely stand for centuries more.

That was the thing about country estates: They stayed in the same bloody place for years.

Of course. That was what she had been trying to tell him.

When Isaac had lost everything, he'd had a Navy pension, and a family to support him, and the ability to find work. Sylvia had survived with none of those. She had tried to build a business, but for whatever reason—luck, skill, market, prejudice—she hadn't been able to make it thrive. What choice did a woman like Sylvia have, but to make herself dependent on a husband again?

She had loved her first husband. At first, anyway. And she'd admitted that their bedsport had been highly satisfactory too.

But love and desire hadn't been enough, because her first husband had let her down.

"Bloody hell," he breathed. "I've got it all wrong."

Isaac's rival wasn't Graham Ossett and his country house. He detested Ossett on principle, but Ossett wasn't the man standing between him and Sylvia.

Michael Ray was. Her first husband: charming, flirtatious, exciting, persuasive, dishonest, disappointing, and dead.

Michael Ray, who promised Sylvia things she never even wanted, and then repeatedly broke his word.

Who ignored her worries and dismissed her fears.

Who poisoned her world against her, then left her to survive in that world impoverished and alone.

The clues had been there, right from the start, if only

he had seen them. When he had rescued her from the tree, she had admitted it: Isaac reminded her of her husband and that was why she didn't like him.

Well, he wasn't like Michael Bloody Ray.

"I love her, and I do know what she needs." He shook his head. "Bloody hell. It seems I'm getting quite an education today."

CHAPTER 22

The Jolly Duck was a coaching inn somewhere on one of the roads connecting Warwickshire to Worcestershire. It was not a particularly charming inn, but Sylvia had chosen it for its name, and now she was stuck here. She could not go forward, but she could not go back, so she decided to stay another night, under the flimsy pretext that the weather might turn.

"Or not," the coachman from Sunne Park said, scratching his head and frowning at the sky. "It might hold for a couple of days yet."

"It's best you take the carriage back to Sunne Park," she suggested. "I can take a coach from here."

But he and the groom refused to abandon her, on the grounds that Mrs. DeWitt and Lady Charles would have their heads. They cheerfully settled into the cozy tavern and set about fortifying themselves with ale and pies. They were known at this inn, they assured her, and the bill would be sent to Sunne Park. That only made Sylvia feel more guilty, as if she were stealing from her friends.

Perhaps The Jolly Duck needed a barmaid, she

thought. Or a cook or someone to distill cordials and flavored wines. She could stay here forever, working for her room and board, and then she'd never have to decide.

Until she lost her position and was back where she started: a penniless widow, now of dubious virtue, with no family and, at the rate she was going, no friends. She had fled temptation for safety, and her safe future still waited, sitting in Kemble Manor, Worcestershire, with a blanket over his knees, a complaint on his lips, and a pointless little cordial in his hand.

As a respectable woman traveling alone, she could not dine in the tavern, but neither could she hire a private parlor when she had little coin and it was her friends at Sunne Park who would receive the bills.

So she sat alone in her narrow room, with a small fire and a plate of toast that she tore into pieces while she prayed, fervently, for bad weather to block the roads.

A flicker of movement outside the window caught her eye. A little snowflake drifted past, and then another. Sylvia dashed to the window, pressed her hand against the glass, and watched the new snowflakes, swirling through the fading light, settling on the ground, each as soft as a kiss.

"Yes," she breathed. She wiped the condensation from the glass so that she could egg the valiant little snowflakes on. "Snow and snow and snow."

Down in the yard, a pair of men strolled from the stable to the main building as if it were a fine summer's day. A wagon pulled up; someone hurried from the kitchen to claim a side of ham and a crate of cabbages, before the wagon driver tipped his hat and set off back down the road.

Then came a lone horseman, riding a hardy-looking bay, snow settling on the greatcoat spread over the horse's back and clinging to his hat. He dismounted in the yard, a dark silhouette, and began to lead the horse toward the stable.

Her breath snagged. Her forehead thumped the glass as she tried to see the figure better. It was hard to be sure, given the dirty window and softly swirling snow, but the newcomer in the greatcoat appeared to be favoring one leg slightly as he walked.

He called out to someone; she could not see who, but that person's response made the newcomer stop. It was the innkeeper, she saw, as he entered the scene. The innkeeper gesticulated at the newcomer.

The newcomer shook his head, removed his hat, and banged it against his leg to dislodge its dusting of snow. Then he smoothed back the long strands of hair from around his face and put his hat back on his head.

Sylvia's heart stopped. Her palm pressed hard against the glass. It *was* him. He had come to find her. Surely, he had come for her.

Just as he had come to rescue her the day she was stuck up a tree, without thought to his own discomfort or the pain in his leg. Just as he had come to her aid at the ball, to fill her dance card, willing to pay the price. What a fool she'd been to ever think him like Michael! Michael only ever cared about himself. Isaac had been a sailor, for pity's sake. He knew what it meant to have other people's lives depend upon him. He kept his promises. He had never let her down.

Not until the end. Not until he mocked Graham and her choices and, like Michael, dismissed her concerns and proved he did not understand her fears at all.

But he had found her.

He said something to the innkeeper, who shook his head and pointed back at the road.

"No," Sylvia said out loud. "No, no, no. You cannot

send him away. Isaac!" she called, but nobody heard. She banged at the window, but neither man looked up. She fumbled to open the stupid thing, but it would not budge.

Isaac was still speaking, his horse stamping its feet. He pointed at the inn. The innkeeper pointed at the road.

They were sending him away, to find another inn.

Sylvia raced out of her room and down the stairs. By the front door, she grabbed a coat at random and yanked it on as she slipped and slid across the yard in her unsuitable shoes, to where Isaac still stood in the snow, hat in one hand. Someone was leading his horse away, into the stable after all, but Isaac stood like a statue as snowflakes settled on his hair.

She said his name. He turned. His eyes raked over her, and his lips twitched, once, twice, and then— Yes! His full smile split his face, and her heart near exploded in her chest.

"You found me," she said. "How did you find me?"

"How could I not find you? When there is an inn called The Jolly Duck?"

"The name reminded me of you."

He turned his hat in his hands. "I feared you had traveled further by now."

"I couldn't bring myself to leave."

"But you didn't come back to me."

"I didn't know what I would come back to."

Snowflakes melted on his cheeks, but his gaze never wavered.

"You would've been coming back to a man devastated by his own foolishness, by his own inability to see what was right in front of his face. You would've been coming back to a man who would give his life for you, because he has finally figured out that you are his life. I'm not letting you go."

She wrapped the stolen coat around her more tightly. "I'm the first woman you've ever been with, so you—"

"Don't," he said firmly. "That's the easy dismissal, and I've dismissed too much for thinking I already had the answers. I thought I only wanted you because you were my first. I thought I enjoyed our time together because it was secret and exciting. I thought it was effortless because there was nothing to lose. But the truth is, I want you because you're right for me. I enjoy being with you because you enrich my world. It is effortless between us because we're perfect together." That vulnerable look entered his eyes, as he stepped closer and clasped her icy hands between his. "I should never have mocked him and said the things I said. I was jealous of him and angry, that he doesn't value you as you should be valued. I'm not asking you to marry me out of charity or gratitude, or because it's easier than finding and courting someone else, or even to have you in my bed, though that's very nice too. I'm asking you to marry me because I love you, and I think you might love me, and we've got a life ahead of us, and damn it all, Sylvia, you and me, we *fit*."

She felt the perfect promise of it, soaring above her; she longed to let her heart soar with it too. But somehow, her feet stayed heavy on the cold, hard ground.

He searched her eyes. "I'm not like Michael."

Her whole body jerked, as if from a blow. He held her steady. Startling tears pricked her eyes.

"I'm not like Michael," he repeated more forcefully. "Don't leave me because he let you down. You know I'll never let you down. You know I'll listen to you, I'll look after you, I'll put your security first. I'll never take a step unless you're taking it with me."

Finally, her heavy feet moved. She shuffled toward him, then her hands were gripping the lapels of his coat. "I'm frightened, Isaac. I'm frightened to make another bad choice. I'm frightened to feel excited, because I don't trust that feeling. I'm scared to let myself dream again. I'm scared to want."

"Then we can be scared together. We can dream together, and we can want together." He cupped her cheek. "I'm sorry I'm so exciting. I can try to be boring for you. I don't know if I can do it, being as dashing as I am, but I can try."

She had to laugh, a shaky, watery laugh. "Oh, I do love you."

The snow was falling more thickly now. Two men called to each other across the yard. Neither moved.

"I've been naive," Isaac said. "But I'm learning a lot fast. We're not at different stages of life."

"I'm older than you."

"I don't care about that."

"I don't even know if I can have children."

"The very least of my concerns. We've both already lived a life, me as a sailor, you as Mrs. Ray, and we're both ready to make a new life. Let's make it together. And whether our life is easy or tough, or grand or small, it will be perfect, if I go through it with you and you with me. What do you say?" He tangled his fingers through hers. "Was this proposal any better than the last?"

"Much better." She stretched up and brushed a kiss over his mouth. "I'm sorry I didn't trust you. I'm sorry I didn't know how to tell you what I needed."

"Some lessons we can only learn by ourselves."

"Then it's safe to say, I've learned my lesson now. I want to make a life with you, and no one else will do."

He was still smiling when their mouths met, in a clumsy, laughing kiss, their lips cold from the icy air.

"Now that's sorted," he said, "what are the chances we can get inside and out of this bloody snow?"

Hand in hand, they hastened back to the inn door and burst inside. The warm air stung her cold cheeks. They helped each other out of their coats, and Isaac called for hot water to be sent to her room.

"If this keeps up, we might not be able to travel for days," Sylvia said.

"Then we'll be snowed in together." That dazzling smile split his face. "What a terrible tragedy. However will we pass the time?"

To: Mrs. Isaac DeWitt

Madam—

Your news proved a great shock to me, which is unkind of you given my worries over my erratic pulse. However, your news is proof that my own behavior these past weeks was fully justified and my judgment sound. And so, without guilt or shame, I inform you that two days ago, the vicar lawfully joined Alice Yates and me together as man and wife. As housekeeper, Mrs. ~~Yates~~ Ossett has proven an immense comfort this dreary winter season, and as wife, she will comfort me all my years. She reminded me that it was you who selected her as my housekeeper, and installed her by my side during your absence, thus effectively bringing our nuptials about. I have therefore graciously elected to bear you no ill will for your perfidy in marrying another.

Yours, etc.

Graham Ossett

Kemble Manor, Worcestershire

SYLVIA SIGHED with relief as Isaac tore the letter from her hands. He ripped it into pieces and flung them out the carriage window to flutter into the road amid the icy slush.

"Have we finished with him then?" he asked.

"Very finished."

"Good. Because we're home."

The carriage stopped and he helped her out. Hand in hand, they stared up at the facade of his townhouse. She loved it already. Her new home.

"It isn't very grand," he said. "But it's ours and it's a start."

"Then we'd best get started."

"Aye-aye, captain," he said, and a moment later, her feet were kicking the air as he swept her up into his arms.

"You keep doing that," she laughed. "Do you mean to carry me everywhere?"

"Only on special occasions." The door opened and he carried her inside. "Besides, you are not tall, nor heavy, and let's not forget this is how it started: me hauling you around like a sack of wheat the day you were foolish enough to get stuck in a tree."

She looped her hands around his neck. "In hindsight, getting stuck in a tree on Christmas Eve was the cleverest thing I ever did."

THE LONGHOPE ABBEY SERIES

Main Series

A Dangerous Kind of Lady

A Wicked Kind of Husband

A Scandalous Kind of Duke

Prequel

A Beastly Kind of Earl

Holiday Novella

A Christmas Affair to Remember

The Brothers DeWitt Bundle

A Wicked Kind of Husband, including A Christmas Affair to Remember

Coming Next

A Sinful Kind of Scot

Each book in this series can be read as a standalone, and the books can be read in any order. As the characters move through the same world, they do appear in each other's stories, but without any overarching plot.

For news on release dates, future books, and more, sign up at miavincy.com/news or visit miavincy.com.

ABOUT THE AUTHOR

Mia Vincy wandered the world for years, sometimes backpacking, sometimes working variously as a journalist, communications specialist, and copyeditor. She always carried a tattered book or three in her backpack, until the advent of the e-reader meant she could carry thousands of books at once.

Mia eventually settled in a country town in Victoria, Australia, to write historical romances, in between bike rides through the countryside and muttering at the walls.

For more, visit miavincy.com.

 facebook.com/MiaVincyBooks

 twitter.com/miavincy

 instagram.com/miavincywrites

Printed in Great Britain
by Amazon

33123851R00115